CONTENTS

G000123890

THE PRICE OF DESIRE

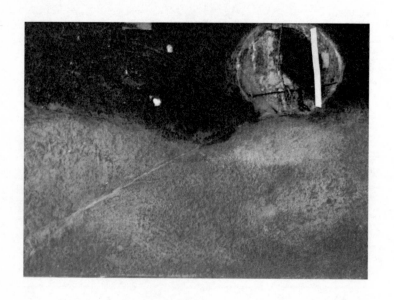

Phyl Herbert

THE PRICE OF DESIRE

ARLEN
HOUSE

The Price of Desire

is published in 2016 by
ARLEN HOUSE
42 Grange Abbey Road
Baldoyle
Dublin 13
Ireland
Phone/Fax: 353 86 8207617
Email: arlenhouse@gmail.com
arlenhouse.blogspot.com

Distributed internationally by
SYRACUSE UNIVERSITY PRESS
621 Skytop Road, Suite 110
Syracuse, NY 13244–5290
Phone: 315–443–5534/Fax: 315–443–5545
Email: supress@syr.edu

978–1–85132–143–8, paperback

The Price of Desire is an enlarged second edition of *After Desire* (2015)

Typesetting by Arlen House

artwork by Nell Graham
grahamnell31@gmail.com

To my three sisters
Peggy, Mary and Eileen

Tell all the truth, but tell it slant
– Emily Dickinson

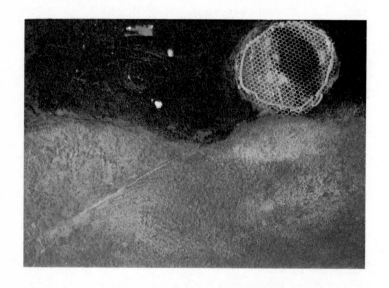

THE PRICE OF DESIRE

LOST AND FOUND

The wheels of the train whistle on the tracks and I leave the city behind. I close my eyes and hope this time it might be different. This time I might be able to talk to her. This time she might listen. The countryside rolls by like a slide-show – sea, open fields, corn and cattle, sheep and horses. I take in the blues, greens, yellows and slip back in time to a world that was black and white, where everything had its place and if there was no place you didn't talk about it. I never talked about it. I told no one, not even my family. Not even my twin.

I get off at the end of the line.

The taxi man knows where the hotel is. Everything is new in this area on the outskirts of the town. We drive towards the coast and I search the landscape for familiar signs, old memories, but the roundabouts have wiped away my childhood map. Somewhere near here I cycled these roads with my cousins during those endless summer holidays. The yellow furze in the ditches – the only trace of childhood – and, of course, the sea. The sea never changes.

'Here we are. The Cliff Edge Hotel, only opened last year. This is as near as I can drive'.

I pay the taxi man and make my way up the narrow path leading to the hotel. It is a big white glassy building with high wooden doors. I'm a woman who falters when it comes to doors. Two wooden panels stretch skywards, there are no handles. I push the wrong side first and then to my surprise, I'm inside sitting in the lobby and waiting on my sister to arrive, my twin sister.

We are coming from opposite directions of the country to spend two nights in this hotel. I've booked some spa treatments for both of us. Bonding time.

I become aware of the voice running in my head. I take a deep breath and listen carefully.

Be nice to her.
She means the best.
Her intentions are good.

I try to repeat the mantra and then I see her struggling towards the entrance, her red travel bag trailing behind her. She frowns back at it as if it were an unruly puppy dog.

'Great to see you', I say to her, my cheek missing hers. She swings around, looking towards the reception area.

'Have you booked me in yet?'

I show her to her room, the one beside mine.

'Let's go for a walk before dinner, I'm stiff from the car'.

She sets the agenda. Even now. She knows that my recent promotion to Head of the English Department was highly-sought-after, but that is of no interest to her. I am still her younger sister, if only by minutes. She came out of my mother's womb as the perfect child, and was the first to receive all of our mother's love.

I walk towards the coffin-lid doors leading to the outside grounds and pull the door instead of pushing it. We walk past the golf links down to the beach. The tide is in. I want to strip off and jump into the salty waves and burn away the barnacles on my skin, but hold back the urge. Her voice rings in my head: 'Not the done thing'.

My sister always knows the right thing to do. We walk until we can't walk any further. A grey boulder blocks our path and we turn back. The light of the evening is fading and we cast a long shadow in front of us as we walk towards the hotel. She looks me up and down.

'Are you changing for dinner?'

'No, I'm quite happy in what I'm wearing'.

'Well, I'm changing'.

I dither at the door before I pull it open.

'I thought you would have learned?'

'If it's not one side, it's the other', I say and surprise myself. She looks at me and I can see she is biting her tongue.

We see a place by the window. A few couples are dotted across the large room. The table settings are more colourful than the diners. A woman scans my body from head to toe. She has that well-fed look, bursting with smugness. A thin-haired man sits opposite her in silence. He is reading his newspaper and playing with the food on his plate. Two women in their forties are seated at the window. My sister points to the table behind them. The waiter comes to us and I am about to order the sea trout.

'She is having the fish and I'm having the steak. Medium-rare, please'.

She also orders the wine. Red, full-bodied. I drink it in, right down to my toes, and feel the wave of alcohol mix with my blood and swish towards my brain. A sea change is beginning.

'This is the life', I say, not meaning a bit of it. I look at my sister and think how on earth did we ever come out of the same womb?

'What more could we ask for?' she responds.

Plenty more, I think, but don't say. We finish the bottle of wine and my sister orders two brandies.

'Your face is red'. She spits out this remark. 'You should have booked the facial'.

'I'm looking forward to the full body massage', I say, and think how I haven't been touched by loving hands in a lifetime. His lifetime, in fact; his twenty years.

She is looking over my shoulder at the two women.

I want to tell her about a morning over twenty years ago when I was leaving home for France. She had come to the house to say goodbye. Then she was a young, married woman, the busy mother of a three-year-old girl. I remember her words.

'You're silly to be giving up your good job and going to France'.

Looking at her now across the table, I try to bring the moment back, to ask her the question I didn't ask then. I open my mouth to speak. Her eyes light up and I'm about to retrace all the years; back to my leaving home with a suitcase packed with lies and deceit and, instead of going to France, taking flight to England to hide my sin and bide my time in waiting.

'Shush', she says suddenly and swivels her head in the direction of the two women. 'You won't believe what they're talking about'.

I leave the table with the excuse of going to the toilet.

I'm sitting in the lobby waiting for my sister who is now talking to the women. The thought occurs to me to go back and interrupt their conversation, but then I see her wave goodbye.

'They're here to get away from everything. They're taking a break before their kids start the Leaving Cert. Thank God I'm over all of that'.

My sister's daughter never gave her cause to worry. She is still the porcelain doll of her mother's creation.

She waves back at the two women who are clinking their glasses.

'Their husbands must be saints, letting them stray away from their duties at a time like this'.

My sister's husband was a saint for most of their marriage until he fell in love with a work colleague and told my sister he had tasted love for the first time in his life and couldn't bear to continue in their cold marriage.

'Do you ever regret the fact you never married?' She is looking at me as she presses the button for the lift up to our bedrooms. 'I suppose your students are your children?'

We step into the lift and I don't answer her question because now she is examining her face in the lift mirror. We get out at our floor and walk towards our separate rooms. She plants a goodnight kiss on my hot cheek. The look of pity on her face pierces my restraint.

'You spent the best part of an hour talking to those two strangers. This break was meant for us to have time together. I invited you here so that we could talk'.

She looks at me as if I'm speaking a foreign language.

'But we know each other. Anyway I'm always interested in what makes people tick. I love getting to know other people, finding out what brings them to places like this'.

I turn my back on her and she shouts after me.

'Don't forget your massage appointment is before breakfast'.

Sleep won't come. I feel a rage creeping over me. It comes in waves. The mini-bar is tempting, but I remember the letter hidden at the bottom of my travel bag and decide against another drink. I turn on the light and look again at the letter, the letter from my son whom I knew and held for only six weeks, the first six weeks of his life. After the nuns found a family for him I returned home to my parents' house. They had believed I was working in France. I resumed my life again as best I could and decided to go to university as a mature student and make something of myself. Then, I thought, I could put the past behind me.

The letter ends: *'Can we meet again? Your son, Sean'.*

I begin to wonder why I feel so stitched into the relationship with my sister. Unravelling the years back to my fictitious journey to France. All this time I thought she'd known I was pregnant and had chosen not to acknowledge the circumstances of my five-month pregnancy that morning I left home. But all along she hadn't known a thing. Or at least that's what I tell myself.

There are some things in life a woman never forgets. The phone number of Sean's birthfather comes into my head again and I ponder whether to ring him or not. Time hasn't blurred the memory of his voice; it still rings in my head after a twenty-year silence. I make the decision not to phone him, not just yet. Best to leave him in his happy marriage.

The soft music and soothing hands of the masseuse ease my body and my mind drifts again into the murky waters of the past. The clouds of those years shift and I see clearly now that I was chasing a dream. The bond between twin sisters is not a given at birth. We didn't share the same soul. We were different. I was always the foolish sister who pined for a closeness where none existed, always looking for trees in the desert.

I dress myself and make my way to the breakfast room where my sister is already seated and reading the morning paper.

'I've ordered you the full Irish'.

'Thank you, but I'm not in the mood today. I've had my fill of the full Irish'.

I call the waiter and order eggs Benedict.

It is time for our last walk together. I stand and let her open the door. The sun is shining and I breathe in the fresh air. I take off my shoes and feel the soft sand comforting my tired feet. A sudden electricity runs up through every nerve end in my body. My feet want to dance. She looks at me with wide-open eyes.

'What was it you wanted to discuss with me last night?'

'It can wait'.

I step out of my old clothes and run into the shimmering waves and remember the clear-blue eyes of my son.

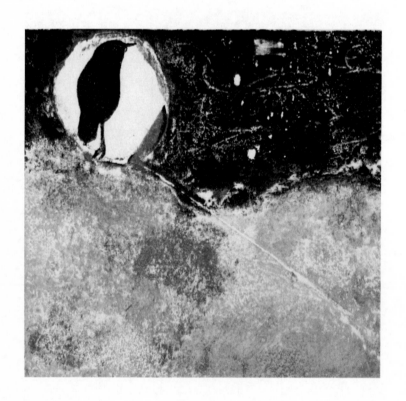

SLIABH NA MBAN

Why didn't you tell me, Kev?

Tom woke and threw his arm over to the other side of the big brass bed. He was waiting for his brother's wake-up nudge. He thumped the space where Kev should be.

The dawn light rode up the dappled-brown wallpaper where the eyes of the Sacred Heart picture stared down at him. A creeping pain ran through him; he couldn't as yet locate it. He sat up and looked out the small bare bedroom window, at the 'Land for Sale' sign sticking out for all the world to see at the front of the house. The November rain lashed against the last few straggling leaves on the ash tree in the small garden. His two-up, two-down house stood alone on the long mile stretch of road. Forty acres divided his land from his neighbours. The house was overlooked by Sliabh na mBan, the Mountain of the Women.

Tom knew it was time to get up and face the day. He struggled to get out of the bed. The face of his dog Rosie drew him to his feet. The dog was lying on his good suit and wagging her tail. Tom pushed the dog off and hung up his Sunday suit, a suit for mass and funerals. Just a few days ago the same suit had provided cover for a different function. Tom had worn it when he had been called in to see the family solicitor, Dan O'Brien.

A matter of grave importance.

Kev was hardly cold in the ground. What matter could be so important? Tom knew everything about the farm. Weren't he and his brother equal partners in everything to do with the land? He couldn't think of anything that O'Brien would have to tell him. He hadn't been prepared for what he heard.

He put on his work clothes, more from habit than need. It was around this time of day that Kev would shout up to him, 'The tae is wet, Tom'.

He would hear him sawing through the thick loaf of soda bread and clattering the mugs on the bare wooden table. These were the sweet first sounds of Tom's mornings for the past sixty years. He had never thought to number those years before, but recent events had claimed the exact count.

The breakfast table was covered with white envelopes. Unopened mass cards that had lain there for days. Who cared who they were from? The deceased wasn't there, pouring his first cup of tea and talking to his brother about the work of the day. Kev's jacket still hung over the back of his empty chair. Tom had no stomach to gather together his brother's clothes and possessions. They could stay where they were for the time being.

Kev had died without any warning. He had passed away in his armchair, his life quenched out. But his death hadn't been the only event unannounced. The matter of a fifty-year-old mystery had surfaced, proving a complete shock to Tom. He had struggled to come to terms with the unravelling of Kev's secret.

'Fifty years, Kev, how could you have kept silent to me?'

Fifty years sieved through Tom's mind in a flash. He had been by Kev's side for every one of them, yet he couldn't exactly put a year on when such a thing could have happened. Days, weeks, years; all had blended into a life of perfect harmony.

Tom had been the younger brother by seven years and had done most of the heavy work. Then, all of a sudden, he began to notice how stiff his brother was becoming. It had been in the blink of an eye, one of those years that he couldn't name. One day Kev was able to climb over the gate to the field where the cattle grazed, and the next he couldn't as much as lift his foot to the first rung.

Kev had masterminded the running of the farm. 'Get that into you. The cattle in the upper field need watering and you need all your strength cycling up that lane-way'.

The O'Connor brothers had had a reputation to be proud about. These days a name could be slurred through carelessness or a word in the wrong direction. They had known the high quality that was expected from their cattle. One hundred head of cattle would be sold to the abattoir in Ennis on a yearly basis. It was Tom's pride and joy to inspect the hide and hoof of each one of them. In the early days they had heard their mother going on about standards.

Don't worry about the fancy machinery', she would say. 'It's the end product that counts, mark my words'.

It was now noon, the time of day when he would usually be returning to the house from inspecting the cattle. Kev would have the spuds boiled with a bit of meat and they would both sit down to eat. Tom would give the news of the morning to his brother, who he had met on the way to the fields and who he had stopped to talk with.

Tom was searching his mind for clues. His brother couldn't help him; he wasn't around anymore to give any answers. Then the memory of one morning, it felt such a long time ago now, came crashing in on him like a tidal wave. It seemed from this distance of remembering that Kev had been in a hurry to get him out of the house. Tom's mind fixed on that morning; he couldn't get it out of his head.

Cycling towards the upper field, he had noticed a red car coming in his direction. He'd stopped to let it pass. It was Nancy Doyle. She must have been in her twenties then.

'Do you like my new chariot, Tom? My days of the bicycle are over. Would you never think of investing? So much easier than the pushing and pulling of that old yoke'.

He remembered his exact reply: 'I'm happy out, Nancy. What use would myself or Kev have for a car? Sure we never go anywhere. This land is our kingdom and you can't take a car on it. A noisy car would frighten the cattle'.

The dog then, a few collies before Rosie, had looked up to Nancy in the car and she'd patted its head for a few seconds.

'Maybe you're right, Tom. A car would deprive this little one of her run up to the fields with you'.

She'd driven back down the road, saying she would call in with a delivery for Kevin. It was the mid-sixties and she'd had a young girl from the town working for her. Her bakery had just won the contract to supply bread to the new supermarket in town.

Kev and Tom rarely visited the town except on Sundays. He remembered one Sunday after Mass saying to Kev, 'The women are admiring me now in my new suit, whether it's to marry me or not, I couldn't say'. He could see Kev throwing his head back and laughing. Tom had only ever had eyes for Nancy, though. He couldn't stop looking at her during Mass. But he knew Nancy had a thing for Kev. He had tried to assure himself back then that Kev had no interest in women and neither did he, that women were trouble. He remembered the cruel tongue of his mother, how her words had cut into his father.

'Can you not stop your mouth, woman?' had been his father's only response.

When he was a small boy he'd overhead his father talking to their neighbour. They were both looking towards Sliabh na mBan.

'Those dark women yonder, they sure cast a shadow over the gable end of the house, but it's a sort of protection too, like the woman inside. You have to take the good with the bad'.

A few years later, their father had died of a heart attack. Tom had been twelve at the time; that was the year he had left school forever. Twelve months later, their mother died from pneumonia. After his parents' death, their bedroom had been closed and neither brother had entered that room again. Or that was what Tom had believed.

In the years that followed their parents' death Tom had not missed either of them. He and Kev had managed very well on their own. They were as close as any two brothers could be; the ideal team. They ate together, slept together and, whenever they went out to town, they stepped out together. They had never argued. Before they went to sleep each night, they would unravel the day's work and tease out any problems, and then thank the Almighty for blessing them with another good day.

Now and again Tom had goaded Kev about Nancy.

'She really has the eye for you, Kev'.

He had loved Kev's reply.

She can have all the eyes she likes for me, I'm not letting any woman into this house – no woman will ever tell me what to do in my own home'.

Words that now made a mockery of Tom's life. His own brother had betrayed him. Anger seized him; he had lost his appetite for food. It was always Kev who'd put the meal on the table after Tom's return from the fields. But bread was the only food that Tom could face now. Bread always made him think of Nancy Doyle. He buttered a slice and put a piece in Rosie's bowl with a drop of soup. The rain was pelting down the chimney. He would light the fire later, when the wind changed its course.

He couldn't get one summer out of his mind. One summer, a lifetime ago. Nancy had returned from a long stay in England. She hadn't been the same Nancy that had gone away. Her parents had told Kev that she had gone away to do a course in hotel management. She had looked pale and she had stopped smiling at Tom whenever he had gone into the bakery. He'd also noticed that she never mentioned Kev's name again, not ever. From that time she had avoided the brothers and Kev insisted that they stop buying her soda bread. But Tom had paid no heed to his big brother. Nancy's bread made him feel warm; the thought that her hands were involved in the making of it played on his mind with every mouthful. He sensed that there had been bitter words between her and his brother.

'I don't think Nancy fancies you anymore, Kev'.

'I'm well rid of that woman, bad cess to her', Kev would always reply. Back then Tom had been comforted by his brother's reply but now it left a sour taste in his mouth.

The light of the day was failing; Tom couldn't see ahead of him. But there wasn't much in his life to look forward to now, it seemed, though he couldn't stop himself from looking back. He thought about the meeting in Dan

O'Brien's office a few days after the funeral. Dan was a trusted solicitor and he'd got to know the O'Connor family well over the years. He had kept it brief.

'Kevin had a daughter who was handed up for adoption'.

Tom's first thought was: how had Kev got time to sire a daughter? Yet that was all beginning to make sense now.

'Well, they're the facts', Dan had said.

'But there's cold comfort in realising the truth of the matter now, Dan. If the girl is claiming that Kev is her father, what can I do about it? I can hardly ask him now, can I? I can't bring him back'.

'There's proof, Tom'. The solicitor was firm.

The woman had turned up on the day of the funeral, three hours before Kevin was put in the ground, and had presented the DNA evidence. It was conclusive, Dan had said.

'She wants half the value of the farm and has claimed her inheritance. I'm sorry, Thomas, but it's the law and it's my unfortunate duty to carry it out. You can still stay in the house, but the land and the cattle have to be sold'.

The face of his mother flashed before him, her words ringing in his ears.

'It's the end product that counts, mark my words'.

Tom put the kettle on and took down a mug from the dresser. Kev's mug hung there and Tom was tempted to throw it on the hard floor and smash it into smithereens. He had always thought there was only one person in the world that he really knew and could trust and that was his brother. Yet he hadn't even got that right. It dawned on him that he was alone now. He had lost his faith in man and beast. Rosie moved from the fire and struggled to walk over to her master. She placed her head on his knees. Tom looked at her honest eyes. Maybe he wasn't entirely alone.

'You're the best pal I ever had, Rosie, faithful to the finish'.

Before going to bed, he surveyed what was left to him. Looking around his kitchen, at the dresser with the shiny red and gold plates standing to attention, he thought 'How bad off am I?' His mother used to say that she had the best crockery set in Ireland; it came all the way from America. It was only taken off the dresser when visitors or the priest paid a visit. Nobody visited now, except the neighbour up the road who called in on pension day. The central plate on the dresser was cracked and glued together in several places. His life was like that now, fractured. He would have to put it back together again, bit by bit.

The 'Land for Sale' sign reminded him now that he would soon be free of the cattle, free from walking up and down the land with his dog, free from bringing the cattle to the market and meeting other farmers, free from doing what he was good at, what he was born to do.

What matter? He had a little patch of ground at the front and the back of the house. The back garden had always been Kev's domain. He'd looked after the drills of potatoes and carrots. Come spring, Tom might grow some vegetables. Maybe he could get a hen or two.

The kettle was boiled for his last cup of tea before bed. Maybe, in time, he might recover from the shock of his brother's death, but the discovery that had come with it was another matter. Tom wished above all that he could talk to Nancy Doyle, but she had sold up years ago after the death of her parents. Rumour had it that she had gone across the sea to America.

The wind rattled the window. Tom got into bed, Rosie at his feet.

HANDS

Officer Tadgh O'Connor was on his last rounds. It was Saturday night. He was thinking of the pint of Guinness that would be waiting for him in The Loft, the nearest pub to the prison. All was in order. His final task was to check on each prisoner through the peep-hole in each of the ten cells on B Wing. So far so good. Most of the men were lying on their beds; some with earphones, others with books, newspapers, magazines.

When he came to cell number ten, he found that the prisoner was in some sort of seizure. At least, that was what it looked like to the officer. The man was writhing on his bed, his arm outstretched towards the ceiling. It was as if the hand didn't belong to him. O'Connor watched for a while, seeing how the man first made a fist of his hand, then shook it about as if he were talking to an imaginary person, or perhaps conducting an orchestra from somewhere in his brain. O'Connor had heard about these types of fits during his period of training. The last entry on his clipboard list read *Cell No. 10: Eddie Murphy*. A Lifer, from the south of Ireland. He knew that Lifers were the ones to watch.

Alice Hayes got off the number eleven bus the following Monday morning. She made her way to the traffic lights at the side of the hospital and proceeded up the entrance to the prison. She rang the bell of the big grey door. The small smiley prison officer was on duty. He scanned her bag with the machine and his eyes scanned the rest of her. 'Little prick', she thought as she walked into the bustle of noise that was the prison community, a living village cut off from the world.

She made her way up the spiral stairs to the upper circle. The first point of call was the teachers' staff room. Monday morning was art, but first Alice needed a strong cup of coffee and a chat with the head teacher who gave her the morning's class list. She noticed that Eddie Murphy's name was missing.

Before the arrival of the men, Alice prepared her room. She organised the materials, paints, brushes, paper, water and easels and placed them on the table along with the unfinished pieces from last week. Eddie Murphy's work was among them. A large sheet of white paper covered with hands. Hands in every position, from every angle; palms, fists, praying. Alice had reminded her class that hands were the most difficult part of the human body to capture in any medium. She heard herself repeating what her own drawing tutor used to say.

'If you master the hands, you've mastered the body'.

Officer O'Connor was summoned to the main office that same Monday morning. The governor put aside his breakfast tray and told the officer to be seated.

'I want your side of the story, O'Connor, and it better be good'.

The officer rolled back the weekend in his sore head. The scene had blighted the past two days.

'It was the last cell I checked on Saturday night. It's all there in the report, governor. Everything was normal until cell no. 10. The prisoner was strange, out of his head. When I entered the cell to ascertain the situation, he punched me in the face. It was necessary to restrain him as per health and safety rules, sir'.

Like a foghorn announcing a new phase of existence, the sound brought all activity in the classroom to a standstill, immediately followed by a stampede out. It reminded Alice of a film she had seen once about lemmings charging into the sea. Coffee break. Four teachers were drinking theirs when Alice arrived in the staff room. A conversation was in high flight about the activities of the weekend. The pre-Christmas rush had begun early, though it was still only the first day of December. The computer teacher was talking about his visit to the RDS. His kids loved the Christmas Craft Fair, but he was shocked at the entrance price.

'That's a load of bollox', said the music teacher.

He thought all kids were spoilt rotten these days and it was far from craft fairs he was raised. The noise in the room rose with the sparring voices between the two men.

During the class, Alice had kept wondering what had happened to Eddie Murphy. Soon enough, the sparring was interrupted by the head teacher, who arrived with news from the governor's office. Eddie Murphy had been admitted to hospital in the early hours of Saturday morning. The circumstances of the accident were not available.

Alice returned to her classroom and her students slowly drifted back to their work. It wouldn't be long now till lunch-time. She wouldn't see this group again for another week and that was too long to wait for news of Eddie. The radio was on; it seemed to Alice that a mix akin to harmony occurred at moments like this, when the class were engaged with their artwork and making progress, music blending with the creative outbursts of colour and changing shapes. That was a thought she had always kept to herself. Christy Moore was singing 'Ride On'.

Pauly, who was another lifer, said, 'that's Eddie's song, he's mad into Christy. He lives near him, near some mad stud farm'.

Alice went to the recess wall that was shelved with unfinished work and took out Eddie's folder. She remembered his first day in the class, just before last Christmas. He wouldn't speak and she had known it would take time for him to settle. He was in no hurry. Sitting by the window, looking out at the yard, was his favourite place in the room. He would look at the same wall for long periods and when a bird landed he would shout out:

'Another fucking seagull!'

'Do you not like seagulls, Eddie?' she had said, and so began the dialogue between teacher and student.

'There's a lot of grey out there. See that wall there with all the barbed wire on the top? How come there's not a tree to be seen?'

Alice knew that prisons weren't built for the pleasure of the residents; this one was surrounded by grey walls and bleak, faraway high-rise flats. Eventually, she'd found a way into his world.

'Do you think, Eddie, you could paint or draw a tree?'

Trees marked the beginning. She got him a Van Gogh print of an almond blossom and put it on the wall near the window over his table. Prison funds were very generous. She was able to order suitable materials. All Eddie's work was dated, week by week, all the Monday mornings over the past year, barring school holidays. He had never missed a class until this morning. She knew what she had to do; she would go to see him during her lunch break.

From trees Eddie had moved to horses. Patricia, the English teacher, told Alice that all his stories were about horses; horses were a vital part of his life. It all came out slowly. Before prison, he had worked as a stable hand in the local stud farm. She overhead him tell the lads in class that he was twenty years working in the same place before he came inside. Alice reckoned that he wasn't yet thirty; he must have been little more than a child when he had left school. He was still a frail figure of a boy, you could hardly call him a man. It was only in the last few weeks, when he'd mentioned to Alice that hands were the method of measurement to assess the height of a horse, that she had suggested a new work. A chapter of hands. His latest project had been a series of Christmas cards, based on his 'hands' pieces.

She told nobody about her intended visit to the hospital. Officers and teachers worked on different sides of the fence. Often she had heard officers referring to teachers as 'do-gooders', a term she despised.

On her way out the main gate, Smiley remarked.

'What a great life you have, only a few minutes ago since you swanned in'.

It was now 12.30. She would have just enough time to visit the hospital before meeting Patricia the English teacher in The Loft for a sandwich.

In the Mater Hospital, the receptionist told her what ward Eddie was in. Imagining she might be asked about the purpose of her visit, she had come prepared. Under her arm was his folder, containing cartridge paper and graphite pencils.

The isolation unit was at the top of the stairs, but she stopped dead in her tracks when she saw the prison officer by his bedside.

'What's your business here?'

Eddie was lying on the bed, his eyes swollen, his two hands in plaster of Paris up to his elbows.

'Can I speak to him?'

'Can't you see he's out of it? He hasn't woken since the operation'.

Patricia was waiting for her at The Loft. The toasted ham and cheese sandwich had lost its appeal but she welcomed the cup of hot tea. Patricia knew something was wrong.

'He was fine on Friday', Alice told her. 'I know that for a fact because he came to my room, looking for more card material. I have to find out what happened to him'.

'Be careful, Alice. You know the rules'.

The afternoon class was small. Two of the men were called out for visits, so there were only three students in the group.

'We've applied to get TR for Christmas, Miss. What do you think of our chances?'

Alice smiled. 'Temporary release has nothing to do with me, lads. You know we're not involved in prison issues'.

'Why not, Miss? Don't you work here?'

That was Deano. He was the one who knew what was going on in the prison; he had all the news.

'Did you hear about Eddie, the guy from the country?'

Dublin prisoners referred to everyone outside of their city as being from the country. Alice played cute. She knew enough at this stage to say very little.

'Just heard he'd an accident and that he's in hospital'.

'He had the crap beaten out of him. The guy in the next cell heard it all. The poor lad was taken out on a stretcher in the middle of the night. Nobody knew who that bastard of an officer was. One of the guys said maybe this will shorten his sentence. Did you know what he was in for, Miss?'

Alice said that she didn't and it was none of her business.

'He shot his brother. His brother was riding his own daughter and she went to Eddie for help. He just got the gun and shot him, shot him dead. Too right too, the bastard had it coming'.

The Loft was crowded. It was Friday evening and Patricia texted to say she would be late. Thirty minutes late. A group of officers, including Smiley, were huddled at the end of the bar. Alice caught him looking at her and whispering something to the others. Uncomfortable, she decided to go outside and wait. Like a flash, it dawned on her that she would have enough time to walk around the corner to the hospital. She wanted to see if Eddie had regained consciousness.

At Doyle's Corner she bumped into two more officers who greeted her politely. She wondered if they knew anything about Eddie. No need to ask the receptionist this time. She knew the ward he was in. But when she got there, another patient was in his bed.

On her way out, she asked about Eddie at the information desk and was told that he had been transferred to Dundrum Mental Hospital for prisoners. She wasn't shocked or surprised – she was furious. So furious she felt like hitting out at the unfortunate young person who had given her the information and shouting to the roof tops, 'how could anyone let this happen?' But instead she just said, 'thank you for the information', and left the hospital.

Her fury had taken her by surprise. It wasn't normal to be getting this involved with a student. Yes, a student; she wouldn't allow herself to call him a prisoner.

When she arrived back at The Loft, Patricia was sitting near the officers' table.

'It was the only free table. Sorry I'm late. Got carried away with shopping. I was trying on dresses for the Christmas party. Do you want to see what I bought?' Alice glanced over at the officers. She didn't want them to see her and Patricia engaged in such girly activity.

'Not now, Patricia. A gin and tonic is what I'd like'.

On their fourth gin and tonic Alice couldn't contain herself any longer. She revealed the story of Eddie to Patricia step by step. She noticed the officers looking over at her. She hadn't realised that her voice had risen several decibels. Smiley passed by their table and hovered longer than was necessary. On his way back from the bar, he placed two gin and tonics on their table. Alice knew she was getting jarred; she also knew that it would be rude to refuse. So she smiled and thanked him. The next move he made surprised both women. He took his chair from the officers' table and deftly placed it opposite the table where the two teachers were sitting.

'Do you know what I'm going to tell ya, girls? Today was the worst day of my life. It really was. Do you want to know why?'

Both women looked at him. The man seemed genuinely upset.

'Why?' Alice, despite herself, was curious.

'My eleven-year-old son rang me up to tell me there was no Santa. Damn it, life isn't the same without Santa'. There were genuine tears in his eyes. 'Can I get you girls another drink?'

Alice jumped out of her seat, not wanting to take advantage of his generosity. She ordered him a pint of Guinness.

The barman gave her the change and said he'd drop it over. Smiley had now moved the conversation forward.

'Do you know something? I'd love yer jobs, ye have it easy'.

Both women laughed.

'Not as easy as you, Smiley', said Patricia. 'What's hard about opening and closing the same door all day long?'

He agreed and put his head back. He let out a giggle that was almost endearing. 'Maybe it's better than the alternative'.

'What's that?' Patricia was drawing him out.

'Working inside with those lads. I did it once, couldn't hack it. So they gave me the door'.

'Literally', said Alice.

He was warming up now, so she tried another question. 'Tell me, do you know what happened to Eddie Murphy?'

Smiley's face changed and he became serious. 'You know that officer has been suspended?' He was about to continue when a big hand slapped him on the shoulder.

'It's your round now, kid. Why don't you leave these young ladies alone and come back to your colleagues?'

The two women shared a taxi home. The taxi drove across town to the other side of the city, where the Christmas lights shone in every tree-lined road and a dazzle of colour lit up their world.

The Visitor

Emma opened the hall-door into her parents' house. She placed her large suitcase in the hall. There was something in the air that caught the back of her throat. It was early morning and usually at this time her mother would have cleared away the breakfast table.

She looked into the dining room and was taken aback to see the remains of the night before. A smell of foreign cigarettes scented the air. The scent of Isobel. Three empty wine bottles stood to attention on the table. Red specks dotted one corner of the white linen tablecloth. There was no sign of life inside the house.

She walked into the kitchen. Looking out the window, she observed her mother and Isobel standing at the bottom of the garden engrossed in the examination of a tall delphinium plant. Isobel was stroking its leaves. The two women began walking toward the greenhouse at the end of the garden, Isobel's arm draped over her friend's shoulder. Emma saw her mother in a new light. Was it something about her face? She couldn't quite put her finger on what it was that was different. It had been a year since Emma and her boyfriend, John, had visited Isobel in her art gallery in Brussels. She had been surprised to hear of her visit to Dublin.

Emma turned up the volume on the radio. The ten o'clock weather forecast was promising a sunny afternoon. Yesterday's phone conversation with her mother came back to her.

'Please darling, will you take Isobel out for a few hours? Take her somewhere with a bit of colour'.

Mount Usher Gardens would fit the bill, Emma had thought. Wicklow, the Garden of Ireland, a good topic of conversation for the drive.

Her mother and Isobel were making their way back to the house and Emma could now see that her mother was wearing make-up and was giggling like a young girl.

'Good morning, pet. I was just showing Isobel our new greenhouse'.

'Looks like you had a good night. Is Dad back on the vino?'

'He had to sample the wine Isobel brought from Brussels. How did your night go, pet?'

Emma had spent her last night in John's apartment. Finally, she had left him after a seven-year relationship. John had thought that their relationship was retrievable but Emma knew different. She had stripped the apartment of her belongings and their relationship of its ties; at least, that's what she was telling herself. Today was the beginning of 'Emma alone, Emma back with her parents'; for the time being, anyway.

Isobel embraced Emma. 'You're a free woman, I hear. That makes two of us'.

'How's that?'

'I've walked out on my life in Brussels, just as an experiment. I left a husband behind'.

Emma wondered how Isobel would cope with life in Ireland. She would be intrigued to see how Isobel would survive not being at the heart of the art world. Surely, she would miss the glamour of her gallery?

'I'm sorry to hear that'.

'Don't be. I'm only sorry that I didn't think of taking this break sooner. Nobody is to blame, except myself, of course. We were never suited'.

A smile spread over Isobel's face, one of those smiles that you could put in your back pocket to warm you on a cold day. Nothing ever seemed to dilute Isobel's exuberance for life.

'Now, you two are going to leave the past behind. Off you go!' Deirdre announced this directive as if she were launching a new ship.

Emma laughed at her mother. 'I have my orders to transport you to new delights, Isobel'.

Driving southwards on the N11, Emma felt, to her surprise, a little giddy. She was now in the company of a woman of the world, a woman who had the courage to flout conventions. The Sugar Loaf shimmered, a blue haze cloaking its slope. Glancing sideways at Isobel she noticed that her mother's friend had put on a pair of sunglasses that covered half her face.

'Isobel never does anything by halves', Deirdre had always said.

Now she reminded Emma of a rock queen in a Shakespearian play she had seen a few summers ago in Regent's Park in London. *A Midsummer's Night Dream*; Isobel was born to play the part of the Fairy Queen. In real life, Isobel's Oberon was George, her senior in the Department of Foreign Affairs. They had met in Dublin.

Emma had always thought it so romantic: the knight in shining armour, taking his love to Brussels the very year that Ireland joined the European Economic Community.

Isobel sat quietly as the motorway opened out in front of them. Emma could feel her looking at her.

'I'm glad you're doing the driving, Emma. It's a long time since I've been on this road'.

'Mam was talking to me about your time in Foreign Affairs. She said the two of you were the wild women of that department back in the seventies'.

Isobel threw her blond head back and laughed.

'It wasn't hard to be wild then, darling. No girl ever grew old in those departments. It was only the spinsters that aged'.

'Don't some girls become spinsters?' Emma said, then realised for the first time she was one herself. She began to wonder how life had been for Isobel and her mother when they were young girls. 'Mam had to give up her job when she got married, didn't she?'

'We were only girls going to the altar. We hadn't a clue about life. We did our growing-up with the help of our friends'.

'Mam doesn't have any friends like you. I mean, here in Ireland'.

Deirdre had lots of friends from the Arts Centre where she worked on a part-time basis, but none of them passed her daughter's scrutiny as suitable companions. Emma thought they lacked sophistication and intelligence.

'There was nobody like her in Brussels either. You know darling, women there are a different breed. Looking back now, I can say that your mother and I were soul mates. It's not often that you come across someone that you can be wholly yourself with'.

'I know what you mean. Except, I don't think I've ever met my soul mate'.

'There isn't one for everybody, darling'.

Emma was a little more than half of Isobel's age but felt ten years older. It was now the middle of her summer holidays, but instead of looking forward to a few more weeks of freedom she felt empty and alone. At thirty-five, she had expected her course in life to be well and truly established. What had she now? No boyfriend, no place of her own. She was at least fortunate in her work; the board of management at her school had awarded her a permanent position which meant that she was paid a full salary during her summer holidays. The job of art teacher in a private school in Dublin 4 was the sum total of her role in life now.

The blue sky was high up and the heat of the midday sun hit off the road in front of them.

'It's so good to see the Irish landscape again. There's nothing quite like it'.

Isobel looked out the window at the squares of fields. 'They remind me of a Van Gogh painting. Crops in their fullness, waiting to be reaped'.

'We're almost there, Mount Usher is the next exit'.

Deirdre opened a bottle of rosé champagne. She had been saving it for a sunny evening. The three women sat in the garden, Isobel at the top of the table, Emma and Deirdre each side of her. The evening held the heat of the day and the flavours from Tim's cooking were drifting into the garden. Without warning, Isobel placed her hands on the arms of both women and exclaimed.

'I've made up my mind. I'm not returning to Brussels. I'm staying here. Experiment is over'.

Emma felt herself becoming giddy again. She looked at Isobel. A warm glow was resonating somewhere between her taste-buds and her elbow, where Isobel had touched her. The heat from Isobel's hand on her skin had sent a charge of excitement that she had never felt before, at least, not in response to the touch of a woman. She looked at her mother and noticed that she too was drinking in Isobel's every word.

'You can stay with us for as long as you like'. Deirdre looked at Emma. 'That goes for you too, Emma. Won't I have my two most favourite women back in my life again?'

'Deirdre, you are such a darling. But I'll be looking out for something'.

'The same goes for me too, Mum', though it had not occurred to Emma to even consider looking for a different place to live. She took it as a God-given right to be in her parents' house. Her home.

Tim had laid the dinner table for the second night in a row. It was a long time since he had seen Deirdre so animated; a spark had ignited overnight. Isobel had brought the house alive. In fact, Isobel was making his own heart beat faster. He was on red alert, fearing he might lose his composure. Tim hadn't always told his wife everything.

He was proud of his menu. He'd designed something that could be left to cook on a slow burner, so he wouldn't have to keep popping in and out to the kitchen. The previous night he had been a bit too fussy with those damned scallops. Tonight he was cooking leg of lamb. Earlier he had doused the meat with a full bottle of red wine. The recipe was a master plan of culinary organisation. Five hours in the oven, then, just before serving, he would add the root vegetables. Isobel had hinted the previous evening, when she had just arrived from Brussels, that she was a meat lady. He would never forget the seductive way she had said, 'I must have my fix of meat dishes'. She had swivelled from the hips and her long torso had done a forty-five degree turn towards him. She had shot the word 'meat' at him and he was reminded of the voluptuous rise of her breasts. She had then settled into the centre position of her chair to take stock of Deirdre's laughing face. Pity that Emma hadn't been able to make it over for last night's dinner, but at least she was here tonight.

It was lamb that Isobel had cooked for dinner that night in Brussels. Tim had booked into the hotel at the airport after his business meeting, but Isobel had invited him to her place saying that she wanted to discuss a problem. It hadn't been clear to Tim what the problem was, but he knew that her husband had also been away on business. He could never have foreseen the aftermath of that evening's meal. Neither he nor Isobel had talked about it since.

But tonight he would be the perfect host. Both Isobel and Emma needed his attention and Deirdre would be pleased with him for taking control of the situation. He would do his best to stay calm and go easy on the vino.

The bottle of rosé was empty.

'Shall we open another before we go in?' Emma looked at her mother for a sign of agreement.

'Let's wait for your dad to join us'.

Isobel stretched her long arms back behind her head, 'I must have a smoke before we go indoors'. She opened her leopard-skin handbag, lined with lilac satin; the tiger lily brooch that Emma had bought her in Mount Usher was sitting on the inside. Isobel took out her packet of cheroots, rolling the long black cigar between her red-painted finger tips. Her lighter was on the table. Emma found herself picking it up, though she had never smoked in her life. She held the lighter towards Isobel's waiting mouth. Isobel took the girl's hand and leaned towards the flame.

Deirdre left the table. 'I must water my little plants before I get too incapable'.

'I'll come too', Isobel got up from her chair and followed Deirdre.

Emma studied Isobel's frame. Her body was still stunningly proportioned; broad shoulders, ample bosom, with a sweeping length of space tapering towards her waistline. Her walk had always intrigued Emma. Isobel had a loose rhythm as she moved, something to do with the languid swing of her hips and the looseness of her shoulders. It was not the walk of an Irish woman, despite the fact that Isobel had been educated in Ireland with the Loreto nuns on Stephen's Green. There was nothing nun-like about Isobel. The woman was a monument to herself.

'What do you do for fun these days, Deirdre? I'm not talking about your work at the centre'.

Emma never heard anyone ask her mother such a question, in fact, the word *fun* and her mother did not at all go together. Emma was even more surprised at Deirdre's answer.

'Tim and I have our moments'.

Isobel laid her hand on Deirdre's shoulder and smiled. 'You'll have to elaborate later, darling'. She looked at mother and daughter. 'Sex is an essential part of life. Once there's a pulse there should be pleasure'.

Emma was in new territory. She remembered her mother's words that morning: 'Go forth and chart new waters'. John had never excited her, not physically or mentally. She knew now, at this remove, that their relationship had seemed to be the bridge that would enable her to leave home. But the fact, Emma realised now, was that she had never been excited by another human being. Not until tonight.

'You must be feeling the chill. Let's go inside. I have everything under control'. Tim was waving the women in.

The light was fading.

The lamb sizzled on the hot plate beside the table.

'Straight to the main course, ladies'. Tim had a hungry audience. 'First things first'.

He poured the red wine, his very best. This was his first year of early retirement and he had decided that as the road ahead wasn't very long, he was going to enjoy every step of it. No point in saving up for a rainy day. God knows, he had spent too many years working as an accountant for that greedy estate agency, Lowry & Son. He was responsible for helping them make their millions, but very little of their profits had ended up in his pay cheque. He carved the meat and served the vegetables.

Isobel made a sweeping gesture with her napkin.

Tim raised his glass. 'Let me make a toast – to all the beautiful women in my life, especially to all those present'. Tim laughed at his little joke.

'I love a man that can cook. I would forgive him any other shortcoming'. Isobel looked enthusiastically on the lamb. 'That poor man in Brussels couldn't boil an egg and there were too many other things he couldn't do'.

'How long were you in Brussels?'

'Emma, darling, it pains me to count the years. Far too many. The only reason I stayed so long was my work in the gallery. I had a few good artists in my stable. I would love to start one here in Dublin'.

'I could help you there, Isobel. I know the scene here'.

Emma felt a sudden rise of energy. Perhaps life had more possibilities than she had thought.

'What do you think, Mam, is the most important quality in a man?'

Deirdre didn't hesitate. 'The ability to be a good friend'.

'I hope I'm more than a friend to you, love. You have lots of those'. Tim smiled again at his quick wit, brought on by more than his usual intake of wine.

'Of course you are love. An intimate friend'.

Emma felt uncomfortable. She didn't like to hear her parents talking about intimacy. After all, they were over sixty, nearly double her age. She looked across the table at Isobel who was twirling the stem of her glass. From her hands to her wrists she was decked in bling, a mixture of coloured glassy stones embedded in silver, her hand movements creating a rainbow of colours.

Tim was replenishing the emptying wine glasses with more than his usual speed. It was probably due to the fact that he hadn't been drinking for a while. He had wanted to give Deirdre and Isobel time on their own. Now Emma was here and he had to be careful. Damned secrets, he thought. He had never hidden anything from Deirdre, but there were some things in a man's life that could not be shared. Events in a man's life that could not be understood. When Isobel had told him that the physical side of her relationship with George had ended, he had taken her in his arms to console her. It was as if some puppet master had choreographed the next stages. They had spent the night together. He looked again at Isobel. But now the memory of her breasts repelled him; he couldn't fathom why.

Tim rose from the table, the thought of his foolishness flooding him.

'Anybody for more food? Plenty left. I'm afraid I didn't make a dessert'.

Emma felt her courage growing; she had lost count of the number of glasses she had.

'I have an idea, Isobel'. The words were out before she could put order on her thoughts.

'Since we're both looking for accommodation, wouldn't it be a good idea if we shared an apartment together?'

A pause fell over the table.

'But darling, what would a young girl like you be doing sharing with an old woman like me?'

Emma was puzzled by this comment. It hadn't really dawned on her that Isobel was the same age as her mother.

'That wouldn't matter to me, we're both free agents', she said a little too quickly.

There was a palpable drop in the temperature of the night.

Deirdre had remained quiet for a long time after Emma's strange request. She had never known her daughter to be so outspoken. Tim opened another bottle.

'Oh, do you think you should?' said Deirdre.

'We're only young once, love', Tim said, winking at his wife.

Laughing, Deirdre gave in. 'That's my boy, Tim'.

The candles had finally collapsed into a formless mess. They had played their part over the two evening meals and were now spent. Deirdre asked Emma if she wanted to drink some water.

'Nobody else in the world would ask me a question like that', Emma could hear the cry in her voice.

'Such a beautiful meal, Tim, thank you'. Isobel rose and as she did, knocked over her wineglass. The rivulets swept across the table towards Emma.

'Jesus Christ, what a clumsy woman I am!'

She leaned across the table in an attempt to pour some of Emma's water over the wine stain. Emma grabbed her hand and tried to take over the mopping. She sensed that Isobel was embarrassed. Emma felt she was back in the saddle again; it was good to see that Isobel wasn't as confident as she pretended.

'A brandy, anybody? Let's have a nightcap?'

Tim tried to bring back the faded glow of the earlier evening but it was too late. The heady mixture of drink and unease had sent their visitor on her way to bed.

'Let me go with you, Isobel', said Deirdre.

'I'm sorry, Isobel, for my daughter's behaviour. I don't know what's got into her'. Deirdre had accompanied her friend to her room. She noticed a shoebox on the bed.

'Another pair? You're still into shoes?'

'You have to see these, darling I couldn't resist them'.

Isobel opened the box and presented the shoes. They were like tiny boats on stilts.

'I bought them in Brussels in my usual place. Aren't they such a work of art? The whore in me couldn't say no. Do you know what the owner asked me the last time I visited?'

Isobel didn't wait for Deirdre's reply.

'She asked me "How is your libido?" I told her that it was as healthy now as when I was a young woman. Then she suggested these shoes. I won't tell you what nocturnal activity she recommended while wearing them'.

Deirdre felt herself blushing, she had forgotten the way Isobel could evoke the shock scenario. In fact, both the footwear and the comments were quite out of place – or was it that they were out of time? It seemed to Deirdre that the shoes were too young, even for her own daughter. Did Isobel really think that she was still in the sixties, still desirable? Deirdre was overtaken by a sense of pity for her friend.

'You do have a most attractive wardrobe, Isobel'.

She couldn't think of anything else to say.

'Look, darling, it's like this. I dress purely to satisfy myself, nobody else. These shoes are for my amusement. Tomorrow is another day'.

But Deirdre had heard enough of her friend's fantasies. She didn't know what to say, what to think anymore.

'I'll say goodnight, love'.

The two women embraced.

Emma was staying in the room beside Isobel's. She thought about knocking on her door to say goodnight, but thought again. She lay in bed for some time, trying to let the room settle. She went back over the day, starting in the lovely gardens of Mount Usher. Isobel had taken her hands and said what a beautiful girl she was and that anybody would be mad not to appreciate her. At that moment, Emma had felt that there was a mutual attraction between them; a definite chemistry. She had even wondered what it would be like to kiss a woman. The bed scene, though, would be difficult for her. Maybe she was losing the plot. In the morning she would put Isobel straight on a few things. If Isobel thought that Emma fancied her, she had it all wrong … Emma drifted into sleep, feeling a vague sense of achievement.

Deirdre undressed and rolled into bed. She felt the heat of Tim's body and was immediately consoled by his presence.

'You don't mind, love, if Isobel stays with us for a while?'

'Of course not'.

He was sure that Isobel had never told Deirdre about the night he had spent with her in Brussels. He had never been aware before that night that he'd felt anything for Isobel. And since then he was sure that he didn't, not sexually anyway. In the morning he would engage Isobel in a conversation about the changing face of Dublin; he would tell her about the rise in apartment living and the growing cultural diversity of the city. He would take her on a tour of the galleries and the shoe shops. He would contact Lowry & Son. After all, they owed him a favour.

FREDDIE MERCURY'S ANNIVERSARY

Nobody knows I'm out. Nobody's waiting. I step out into the world. The sun hits the roofs of the parked cars. I see the shiny black one, just like the picture I have in my black plastic bag – the only one that stayed on my wall for the entire six months.

'Fuck the Rich' was scribbled across the side of a big juicy black Jag. 'Fuck the Poor' as well – I'm not going back to poor anymore. No, Ivy girl, this is the first day of your new life.

Can't face the filthy flats, so I take a wander up the North Circular Road. The same as ever, but different. Inside, your eyes see only as far as the walls of St Patrick's where them mad young fellahs are locked up. Inside, you see the short row of cells. I'm dizzy, giddy, looking at the long shaky lines of houses, shops, cars; people buzzing out in front of me. I put my hand in my freshly ironed blue jeans to check my money. Fifty smackers. Tomorrow I'll sign on. Today

I'll ramble. Get my head together. Let my eyes take in the long streets, turn the corners, see where they lead me.

At Doyle's Corner I see my scumbag of an uncle across the road. I sneak into a doorway, don't want him to know I'm out. He's on his way to the pub where he drank with his wife every night of their married life. She's dead now. Run over by a posh black car. The driver scarpered. She was brought off in an ambulance. They'd had a row in the pub. She ran out across the road; he stayed on drinking.

I wrote a poem about her in my English class. The only good thing about prison is the school there, the teachers.

He's gone. Feel like a good dose of fresh air now to clear my lungs, to get the dirty image of that sleazebag out of my brains.

Turn right at the traffic lights. Steer clear of the shopping centre. Ivy, remember what happened there last Christmas. All in the past now, girl. You'll never stoop so low again, not now. Not when your sights are aimed at big things, new beginnings.

Shopping centre is behind me now. Two roads. Which to take? One leads to the Botanic Gardens, the other to Glasnevin Cemetery. Will I say hello to Ma? Not today, Ivy. This is not a day to depress yourself.

Oh God! Why wasn't I born in a house like that? A big red-bricked house. My little kip of a flat would fit in the porch. A couple, all lovey-dovey, stop outside in their big flash car. I feel like screaming, 'What are ya looking at, I'm as good as you lot'. I was just born into the wrong fucking family. Stop now, Ivy, that's no way to talk. Remember what you learned in the school.

Think positive, think in poetry.

Nobody is going to look down on you again, and that's a promise Ivy.

The sun hits my face. I look up. No clouds. All is clear up there in that blue sky. A good omen. Breathe in, girl. In through the gates of the Botanic Gardens, I take in all the colours in front of me. Reds, pinks, yellows, blues; the colours of the rainbow, all splashed about on the green grass. Further away I see the big fancy glasshouses. I'll leave them for another day.

The colours take me back. I'm twelve again. Mr Kinsella was the first male teacher I had after the nuns. My first year in secondary school. He brought us up the mountains in a bus; he gave out boots and a small bag for our lunch. My Ma was sick, so I had none. We had to climb the mountain. I couldn't lift my feet; the boots were huge.

He came behind me and gave me a gentle little push. It was like as if he gave me wings. I was up the mountain like a bird in flight. He helped me to cross a river. When we got to the other side he called me over.

'Look at that sight, Ivy, did you ever see anything like it?'

My heart made a little jump. There in front of my eyes was a big spread of bluebells. No green grass, only blue; everywhere, blue. I swear to God I nearly cried at the beauty of it all. He was the best teacher I ever had until the school inside.

Inside a building on the other side of the gardens are people sitting at tables, eating, drinking. God, I'm starving. It's twelve o'clock. We'd be having our lunch inside now. Tuesday, it would be cottage pie and peas, and apple tart and custard. What wouldn't I give for it now? I scrunch my plastic bag tighter, squeeze it under my arm. Join the queue. Put coffee and a scone on my tray.

'That's five euro', the cashier says.

Daylight robbery, I think but, of course, I don't say it. Sit down at a table behind four girls. Put my black bag under the chair. Listen to their chat. One of them, just back from a weekend in Paris. She fancied a break there and just took off. The other one, opposite Miss Paris, got new wheels over the weekend.

'See it over there', she says. 'The black Mini Cooper. Daddy gave it to me for my twenty-first'.

My heart is thumping. I press the key-button and the little Magic Mini sings to my touch. I turn left and away, away up the hill with no destination in mind. Jesus, that was easy. When they were all looking at the Paris photos I leaned over to pick up my plastic bag and Mini Cooper's handbag was right under the chair. Pulled up the two in one sweep under my arm and took off like a mad thing. Ivy, you're a scream.

I start to sing. The road flits by as I drive on. I leave the city behind. Shit, a red light flashing? Not taking any chances, turn into the next petrol station and put in twenty euro's worth.

The world is your oyster Ivy, where to?

It strikes me I've never been outside of Dublin. I see a sign for the airport; I follow that. Not enough money to fly away, so I decide to follow the lane that says Belfast. Ivy girl, this car is a beaut.

Turn the radio on, Freddie Mercury belting out his big notes, 'Don't Stop Me Now!' Can't believe it's Freddie Mercury's anniversary today. Ivy, you're on a roll, another good omen. My hero, Freddie, is looking out for me. He's up there with my Ma. Jesus, now they're only playing 'I'm in Love with My Car'. My car. It is now. Fuck that cow, Daddy can buy her another one.

Da's, you wouldn't know about them things, Ivy, would you? Don't think your Ma even knew who your Da was. Never got the chance to ask her.

Jesus, what's this ahead? A toll gate. *Have your exact change ready: one euro and seventy cent,* the sign says.

I hand the woman in the little hut two euros, she looks fed up. Start up again and a big fluorescent sign catches my eye. 'Arrive Alive'. Not thinking of dying yet, too much living to do. Where to now? Might as well follow the road to Dundalk.

I see a cop on a motorbike in my rear mirror, he's looking directly at me. Cool it, Ivy, your imagination is playing games. He passes. Need to stop, get off this road, use a toilet, stretch my legs. Shops coming up, slow down, park, lock car. My legs ache, my head is lifting.

'Cup of coffee please', I say to the barman. 'I'll be back in a minute'.

'Three euro', he says.

I gather my thoughts. It dawns on me that I don't know where I'm headed. Not really. Don't know what the fuck I'm doing?

What would be happening now in the Joy? Four o'clock. School over. Laundry or visits. Nobody ever came to visit me, afraid they'd pick up something. One bitch of a screw called me 'Poisoned Ivy'.

Back to my mini. Drive out towards the motorway. There was only one of my Ma's fellows that I liked. Jimmy was his name. He used to drive a taxi and when he was waiting on my Ma, he'd take me for a spin. One day he asked me would I like to learn how to drive.

'Some day, Ivy', he'd say, 'You're going to be one hell of a driver'.

Thanks, Jimmy, that day is today.

I'm out now on the motorway and, God, I don't like what I see. A big long endless streak of road, nothing either side. It's going on into eternity. Ivy, you better think fast. Mammy, please help me.

My First Communion comes into my head. The nuns were teaching us about sin, and saying that heaven was a place that went on forever and ever and into eternity. That's where I learnt that word – eternity – forever and ever, no ending. That night, I couldn't sleep at the thought of anything going on forever and ever. I didn't like the idea of heaven after that.

I'm getting this flash, it's from my Ma. I know now what I have to do. I have to go and see her. Turn back, the road back is easier.

I stop the car outside Glasnevin Cemetery and find a parking space. I'm dizzy from all that driving and concentrating. My top is sticking to me. I'd love a shower. Walk past the monument in Glasnevin. Her grave is just around the corner, near the taps. The one with the wooden cross on it, no headstone, nobody to carve her name with pride. Except me.

'I'm sorry, Ma. I promise I'll get a nice big headstone some day and I'll put your name on it. Did you remember, Ma? It's my birthday today. They let me out before my time was up'.

'I'm sure, Ivy, you'll be having a big party for your twenty-first', the screw sniggered at me.

I bless myself. I know what I'll do, Ma. I'll get you a bunch of flowers and the two of us can sing 'Happy Birthday'.

At the gate, I spend my last twenty smackers on two bunches of flowers. One for you, and one for me. Red roses for me and pink carnations for you.

Shit, they've clamped the Mini Cooper. I stand and look at the yellow gates that have trapped the little black wheel. That's you snookered, Miss Mini. I walk across the road and back down towards the North Circular Road. The road back is easy. I'm back where I started from this morning. Two roads, which to take?

Brave Inca

'A euro each way on Celestial Bliss and a euro to win on Brave Inca. Is there anything else madam would like?'

Annie kissed herself in her small mirror, then carefully twirled the top back on her red lipstick.

'No, pet, I have the lunch in. Vegetable soup again today'.

She was nearly at the end of the bag of bruised vegetables she'd bought for half-price in the corner shop four days ago.

The post clanked onto the hall mat. A brown envelope addressed to:

Jack McGrath
6 Pleasant Cottages
Dublin 7.

'I'll open this after I place my bet'.

'And not until we see the results of the 3.30', she smiled back at him.

Annie knew his routine during Cheltenham week. It was morning bets, lunch and then sitting down in front of the telly, imagining that they were there with the punters in the stalls. Jack always had the odd flutter on the gee-gees but he was a cautious man, particularly now as money was scarce. Annie loved the odd flutter herself – well, it was more than the odd one, she ran a Lotto syndicate twice a week with a few of her neighbours. Two euros per week; one for Wednesday, the other for the Saturday draws. They were never lucky; they'd had one win of five euros divided four ways, over a year ago. All of them believed that one day their numbers would come up, just as Jack thought his horses would come in.

Jack no longer worked at the garage.

'The world is your oyster now', his boss had said when he had given him his last pay packet. 'You might pick up the odd nixer here and there but at your age you should be taking it easy'.

What Jack's employer really meant was: *there isn't enough work for you*. It wasn't the first time Jack had been laid off due to lack of work, but this time it was permanent.

The younger mechanics knew all about computer operations in the garage. Jack, though, was old-fashioned; he thought he knew cars inside out, but technology defeated him and so did the new push-button engineering. It was now a year since his final pay packet and as for *picking up the odd nixer*? The odds were against him; there were very few old cars on the road these days and Jack would have to wait another year for his pension.

They watched the horses being led around the Parade Ring. Jack pointed out his two hopefuls. Annie was looking at the glamorous women in the Grand Stands. She had always had an eye for style and could make a cheap colourful scarf from Oxfam cut a dash over one of her well-worn jumpers. Celestial Bliss came in first, but unfortunately he was minus his jockey, while Brave Inca fell out of view seconds after the start of the race.

'It's not a fair race. Shouldn't it be about the horse and not the rider?'

'No, love. No good without the weight of the jockey on his back'.

Annie kissed Jack on the cheek and got up to clear away their lunch dishes.

The letter from the department dealing with pensions stated briefly that Jack was not eligible for a contributory pension due to insufficient prepaid stamps. He would have to be means tested for a non-contributory one.

'Are they looking for blood? "Means tested"? I've never got a penny from any one of them, never even drew the dole when I was laid off'.

'You could have drawn the dole over the years if you weren't so proud'.

'Not when I was doing nixers, Annie. No dole and no bus pass. That'll probably be axed by the time I'm due it, knowing that present shower of muppets'.

'Don't be too hard on them, Jack. Didn't you make a few bob out of them when the garage had the contract for their cars? In anyway, next year we'll both have the travel pass and we can swan around the country for nothing'.

'We'll be swanning around the country before that, love, and that is a promise'. He rolled the letter into a ball and kicked it into the bin.

The garage Jack worked for used to have the contract for the fleet of ministers' cars and Jack had been the appointed and approved mechanic. He knew his way around Government Buildings – or at least, around the government car park. Until last year, when the garage had lost the contract and Jack had lost his job.

The next morning he rose at dawn, just as the birds were beginning to sing. After bringing up Annie's morning cup of tea with a note perched on the edge of the saucer, he left the house without a sound. It was 8am when she woke. She drank the cold tea and read the note:

Be ready for the big open road at ten
We are in luck
We'll be setting off South
with the lend of a Benz.

At precisely 9am, Jack left Government Buildings, driving a wine-coloured Benz. The security man knew him of old and asked no questions. He drove the car carefully back to his house. When he opened the hall door, he could hear Annie singing in the kitchen.

'Your chariot awaits you, madam'.

Annie looked out the window and wondered if Jack had won the Lotto on the sly.

'Where would madam like to go today?'

Annie knew that her husband had been plotting something but she hadn't been sure what; she was determined to go along with his plans, whatever they were. It wasn't an unknown event for her. During those years when Jack had been occasionally laid off from the garage, he used to service the odd car in the laneway at the back of their house and, every now and then, a customer would loan them a car for the day. Years ago, when the kids were young, they used to spend a whole day in Bray, getting there in a borrowed car, riding on the amusements and feasting on candy floss. The kids were in Canada now, all three of them. Only Jack and Annie now.

'Bray, Jack; that's where I'd like to go'.

'Bray it is, so'.

They drove out of town towards the N11 and arrived in Bray in no time. Before they got out of the car, Jack asked Annie to open the glove compartment and take out a package. It was wrapped in red paper. Inside was a red beret and a silk scarf to match and pinned to the beret was a turquoise brooch. A seahorse, her favourite creature in all the world. She put them on and kissed Jack.

'It's not my birthday, you know?'

'Every day is your birthday from now on'.

He opened her side of the car and they both sauntered along Bray pier. Annie was in her element with the sea breeze on her face and Jack on her arm.

It was 5pm when they arrived home. Jack said he was going to return the car before evening set in. She didn't ask him where he had got the car or, for that matter, the money to buy her presents. She knew he would tell her all later.

Maisie Byrne knocked on Jack and Annie's door. It was the following morning and the house was silent. She looked up at the bedroom window and noticed that the curtains were still drawn.

'Love birds', she smiled to herself. Imagine at their age. No wonder Annie had been all dolled up yesterday on her way back from her day out. Maisie dropped her two euro piece, wrapped in her Lotto numbers, into the letterbox.

The sun swam into the bedroom when Annie pulled open the curtains. Jack was still asleep. The rush of excitement from yesterday's pranks had taken all of his energy. Several times during the night she had heard him muttering, 'I'm a cautious man'. She would give him a sleeping tablet tonight. She had never known her husband to be so restless.

Ms White walked into the cul-de-sac called Pleasant Cottages. It looked like a scene from a children's fairytale. A semi-circle of little dolls' cottages; small front doors, one window up over the door and two down. She wondered where a family would fit in such a tiny house? It reminded her of that nursery rhyme:

There was an old woman who lived in a shoe,
She had so many children she didn't know what to do.

How much property tax would they pay on a little box like this? And water tax next year? How did they do it? It was, of course, none of her business, she told herself. It was her job; what she was paid to do. She knocked on number six. Annie answered.

'I'm from the Department of Social Welfare and I'm here to see Jack McGrath'.

Jack was one of those rare Irish men who didn't have a taste for alcohol, but after Ms White left, he took the bottle of whiskey from the cupboard in the kitchen. It was still half-full after the Christmas visitors. He had been keeping the rest for Paddy's Day, but this was more important.

'Sit down, Annie, *mo ghrá*, love of my life, and join me in a toast to our future plans'.

He poured both of them a measure.

'There are some actions in life a man has to follow through on for the sake of his dignity. You do understand I couldn't do a blessed thing without you by my side?'

Annie knew she had to go along with whatever plan her husband was plotting. She was beginning to see him in a new light, her man of action. She was excited. He had always done the right thing by her. Two items were produced magically from his pocket. The first was a map of Ireland; the second, a poster of classic cars.

'Let's decide on two things before we drink. What part of Ireland will we visit tomorrow?'

He lay the map and the poster across the table. Annie pointed to Galway.

'The City of the Tribes. I've never been there'.

'And what car would madam like as her chariot?'

'Not a Benz, Jack. We did Bray in that and it was like a bird in flight, a bit too fast for me. I like the look of the Porsche'.

'Whatever the lady desires, she shall have'. He poured the remainder of the whiskey into a hip-flask and put it into his coat pocket.

'For tomorrow', he said.

'Dare I ask who is giving us the loan of the car for this trip?'

'Wait and see, my love. It will all be revealed in good time'.

Jack had told Annie that the car for Bray had been loaned to him by a person that owed him a favour – and that there were plenty more motors where that one had come from.

The next day was St Patrick's Day. The city had come to a standstill except for the parade. On their way into town, they bumped into Maisie Byrne. A huge sprig of shamrock was making its way up under her chin. She looked Annie up and down.

'Not sporting the Green today?'

Annie was a dazzle of red; as well as the beret and scarf, she was wearing the red earrings that Jack had bought her in Bray. Maisie noticed that Jack was wearing a name tag underneath his striped scarf. It looked like it was part of a necklace.

'Off again on a skite, where to this time? I hear there's a fancy dress party on in the Mansion House'.

'We're in a hurry, Maisie. See you later'. Annie waved her friend goodbye.

'Nosey old cow, that one. Tell her nothing from now on', Jack said.

Drums and trumpets sounds were in the distance. They walked down Dorset Street and turned the corner towards Parnell Square. The bands were getting louder and it was starting to be a struggle to get through the crowds.

'What an Irish stew'. Jack couldn't understand what there was to celebrate about being Irish; not now, particularly when the country was going down the plug-hole. A man was sure of nothing, not even his pension. A tall sign for the Bank of Ireland caught his eye. Written across the top of it was: WE CARE FOR OUR CUSTOMERS.

'Like hell they do! Not little people like you and me, Annie'.

Jack and Annie had no need of banks. Their small savings account in the post office was down to the last few euros. He pushed his way past the throng, holding Annie by the hand.

It was no time before they had walked up O'Connell Street. They made their way towards Trinity College, down Nassau Street, and turned around the corner into Merrion Square. They passed the National Gallery and Jack took off his scarf and handed it to Annie. He pinned his name-tag outside his coat and they entered Government Buildings.

'My partner in crime', Jack said to the security man, who laughed and watched them both walk towards the ministers' car park.

It was three o'clock in the afternoon when they approached the last roundabout before Galway city. The tail end of the parade there delayed them for a few minutes. Annie admired the young majorettes flipping up their batons in the air. Another young one, dressed up in a ban garda costume, knocked on the window. Jack told her to go back to the parade; he was in no mood for games. She asked him for his driver's licence and proof of ownership of the red Porsche. Jack was getting more than a bit impatient with this young girl. The last baton-throwing majorette passed.

Jack put his foot down and took off with the speed of a Nigel Mansell.

'Let's take this minister for a ride'.

Annie held her tongue; she had never seen Jack behave like this.

He drove through another roundabout but, instead of going towards Galway city, took the road out to Connemara.

The roundabouts were making him dizzy. He let out a sigh of relief when they came to the open road with the sea on their left. *Failte go dtí an nGaeltacht.* A big sign marked a change in territory.

'That reminds me of the sign in that film *The Guard.* Wasn't it made somewhere around here?'

'You're on the ball, Annie, and we're coming into the very place. Spiddal'.

He stopped the car and turned in towards the sea. The tide was in and the waves were licking their way towards the shore. Annie looked out at the Atlantic Ocean; she could see the Aran Islands in the distance.

'I'd love to go there, Jack'.

'Some day soon. Let's have one more for the road, Annie'.

He reached for two small glasses from the glove compartment and handed his wife a pill first and then poured her a measure of whiskey from his flask. There wasn't another soul on the pier at Spiddal, but in the near distance they could hear the sirens of speeding cars.

'Hold my hand, Jack. I know they'll never catch up with us'.

Jack looked at his wife.

'My Brave Inca, my dearest Annie'.

He put his foot down and drove the length of the pier and beyond.

LUNAR LADIES

Her tea-trolley is set. The cups are placed upside down, on saucers stacked on plates. Bonnie's Sunday soirées are an event written into the social calendar of the many women of her acquaintance. But this Sunday is different. It is the Sunday before the New Year and only her two best friends are invited. Ester and Hilda are devoted to Bonnie, but not necessarily to each other. Attachment to Bonnie is what they have in common.

The bottom shelf of the trolley hides the sweet delicacies that will follow the egg sandwiches. Bonnie looks in the big gilt-framed mirror, pins back the grey curl on her forehead with a silver slide and adjusts her dark glasses. She scans her figure from head to toe; she is wearing her favourite dress, given to her by Hilda. The two women have known each other since they were young women. Bonnie's first – and only – job was as secretary to Hilda's husband, Henry Kelly, in the firm of Kelly, Fitzgerald & McGrath, Solicitors. Twenty years later, Ester was to work in the same firm, and that was how all three had met.

The knitted royal blue wool dress fits snugly on Bonnie's four-foot-ten frame, covering the pronounced stoop that she has always endeavoured to hide from view. Pink pom-pom slippers complete the outfit. She smiles at her reflection. The doorbell rings. It takes her some time to move across the room.

'Coming', she says. She lifts the phone on the wall of her living room and presses the buzzer.

'Hope I'm not too early?' Hilda kisses Bonnie on the cheek.

'I'm more than ready, Hilda. What a smart suit'.

Hilda places her fur coat carefully behind the white settee and hands Bonnie a small box.

'A few éclairs for later'.

The low table in the centre of the room is covered with paper cuttings of theatre reviews and a green leather-bound diary which contains Bonnie's meticulous daily entries, secret to everyone except Bonnie. The afternoon light slants through the broad windows of the living room. It is an old, purpose-built apartment block, one of the first built in Dublin, not far from the sea in Dún Laoghaire.

The bell rings again and Bonnie lifts the phone. 'Come in if you're good-looking'.

Bonnie and Ester embrace each other.

'We're all here now', Bonnie says. 'That time of year thou may'st in me behold! Sonnet No 73'.

She makes this pronouncement as if she is about to say Mass. Bonnie may be small, but she engages in dialogue as though she were projecting from a stage.

'You look terrific, Ester. You're getting younger-looking. I swear to God, I don't know what you're doing to yourself', Hilda says this almost accusingly.

Ester looks in the mirror. 'I have to say, folks, I'm sorry I didn't go blonde years ago. Whoever said youth is wasted on the young was right'.

'You're dead right there, Ester', Hilda laughs. 'Back in the day, I was such an innocent that I didn't even know I was either young or good-looking. What sort of eejit was I?'

'You're still looking great, Hilda', Ester looks approvingly at Hilda's tweed suit.

'Will you stop fooling yourself! When you get to my age the hairdressers have only one style for you and that's the cauliflower head of curls'.

'Hilda, you have to demand more'.

Hilda throws her eyes up to heaven.

'Are you playing any tennis these days, Ester?' asks Bonnie.

'Yes, I had a game this morning. My second this week. I'd play more often if I could. But tennis is like sex – you can't do it alone'.

Ester looks at Bonnie for a response. She knows her friend, despite the years, is still partial to the double entendre.

Bonnie smiles. 'Exercise is important, Ester, and so is pleasure'.

'Pleasure?' Hilda snorts a laugh. 'Sure, I didn't get any pleasure out of mine. I never knew which end of me was up. Don't ask me why I bothered marrying either of them'.

Hilda has seen two husbands to the grave. As a young girl, her dark looks were compared to those of Sophia Loren; she and her sister were always the first to be invited up to dance in the Metropole Ballroom in O'Connell Street. But her dancing days were short-lived. Her first marriage to Henry took away her ballroom evenings and, after giving birth to three children in quick succession, her likeness to Sophia Loren soon faded.

'It was the thing to do back then', Ester declares. 'Getting married'.

'You never got caught, Ester'. There is a touch of envy in Hilda's voice.

'No, and look where it got me. My head was always in the moon. I don't know where my forties and fifties went. What was I doing for those years? At least you have your children and grandchildren'.

'How are the boys, Hilda?' asks Bonnie, changing the subject. Bonnie has known Hilda's sons since they were born. She had babysat them when they were little and knew every beat of their lives. She loved Hilda's boys as if they were her own.

Hilda thinks to herself about her sons. Not boys anymore; both men in their forties. Two men, totally devoted to their wives.

'They're grand', she says.

The three women sit for a while in the centre of the living room, drinking in the atmosphere. The apartment was left to Bonnie by her aunt and uncle over forty years ago; they were both Abbey actors and the room is a shrine to their memory. Framed photographs line up a gallery of remembrances. The walls are green. Bonnie likes to call it her green room. Ironically, the phrase now has real meaning for Bonnie, because it has become, in fact, her backstage room. She doesn't enter out anymore, not since she got her stroke a year ago. The acting heroes look down from every side of the room. Three white sofas surround the low table.

Bonnie rises from her seat. She is about to perform the tea ritual. Ester moves to follow Bonnie to the kitchen but Hilda cautions her back.

'We have to let her. It's her party and her kitchen'.

There is a silence between the two women now.

'How did your Christmas go, Hilda?'

'Mother of God, I'm glad it's all over. I was stuck in a corner at James's table and I thought I'd never get home'. Hilda is indignant. 'Do you know what they gave me? A single cup and saucer wrapped up in fancy paper with a blooming big bow on it. Now if that's not a reminder that I live alone, I don't know what is. I can't wait for the New Year'.

'Well at least you had company ...' Ester starts, but stops as Bonnie comes back, pushing her trolley to the centre of the room.

Hilda turns the three cups onto their saucers and Ester pours the tea. The egg sandwiches are eaten and, as always, someone says, 'Bonnie you make the best egg sandwiches in the world'.

The china cake stand at the bottom of the trolley is decked with Hilda's chocolate éclairs and Ester's Swiss roll. Both have to be sampled. Hilda takes a bite of chocolate éclair and looks at Bonnie. 'It's only here that I allow myself the pleasure'.

The three women laugh.

'Did you see Nigella last night?' Bonnie looks at her two friends.

'No. What was she cooking?' Ester is curious.

'I don't give a fig for what she cooks', Bonnie says forcefully. 'I just love looking at the sheer physicality of her performance. She makes me feel hungry'. Bonnie realises she has said too much and falls silent.

It is ten years since Bonnie's partner died. Ester and Hilda always referred to Nuala as a 'part-time lover' because they had never met her. Bonnie was the one who used to travel to London on a regular basis to be with Nuala, never the other way around. Each visit was a mixed blessing for Bonnie, as she would swing between euphoria in London and depression on her return to Dublin. Gay women were an underground movement in the Dublin of that time.

But Hilda and Ester are used to Bonnie's appraisals of attractive young women. Last year, it was a young actress who performed in a lunchtime play in Bewleys. Bonnie had travelled into town every day to see the play. Since her stroke a few months ago, however, she has become housebound; this year the objects of her desires are television personalities.

'Can I read out my poem before we start?' Ester searches in her big red handbag. 'It's called *Archaeology of the Soul*'.

'Archaeology … what has that got to do with the soul?' Hilda is puzzled.

'The past', Bonnie says authoritatively.

'Can I begin?' Ester sits up straight and takes a deep breath.

At the funeral of my youth
Only one offered a cushioned
Grave for my remains.
'Will you marry me?' he asked.
'No', I replied, and then I died.

'I know who you're talking about, Ester', says Hilda. 'That gay fellow. You had a lucky escape, believe me'.

'Stop it, Hilda. Finish the poem, Ester', Bonnie urges.

Now I am the big Oh …
And have opened up myself on the shelf.
Have babies and catch up on myself.

'My God, Ester, are you mad?' Hilda stares at her. 'How on earth could you have babies? At your age?'

Ester is uneasy at her revelation. Nobody needs to point out to her that the tide of time has fast run out on her. She spent over fifteen years living with a man who wasn't interested in the sexual side of their relationship. It was her own fault that she remained with him, but she had liked him. A weak excuse, she knows, but he had made her laugh.

'I know what age I am, Hilda. It's just my fantasy. You don't get it, do you? A girl can dream'.

There is an awkward silence. Bonnie stands, breaking it. 'Now to the business that we've all been waiting for'.

Bonnie takes down the portrait of her aunt and uncle and turns their faces to the wall. Behind the portrait are sellotaped three sheets of paper. She passes a sheet each to both women.

They all read in silence.

'Jesus, Mary and Holy St Joseph', Hilda mutters. 'If my boys knew I did this, they'd have me certified'.

'But we do it every year'.

'Ah Hilda, you're not dead yet! So who's going to read out their wishes first?' Bonnie is taking control, as she always does.

'Right, I will', says Hilda. 'My number one was to lose weight and get more exercise. Well I didn't do too well there, I'm still the same tuppence ha' penny. My number two, to learn how to please myself more. My number three, to get away more often, while I still can'.

'You did very well, Hilda. Haven't you been away tons of times?' Bonnie says.

'Yes, but not with people I like. It was like being back at school, being told where to go and at what time. I didn't enjoy a bit of it. I only went on those trips because the bridge club needed to make up the numbers'.

'There was no pleasure in it for you, Hilda', Bonnie pronounces.

'Pleasure', repeats Ester. She plays around with the sound of the word on her lips. 'That's what it's all about. Pleasure'. She laughs and turns to Bonnie. 'Read out yours'.

'I'm still hosting my Sunday afternoons and inviting people I've known over the years who have touched my life. My second wish was travel, but unlike Hilda, I can't do that. Thank God, though, I still have my imagination. I can travel in my head, can't I?' Bonnie chuckles, suddenly embarrassed.

'That's two wishes. What about your third?' Hilda asks.

Bonnie drops her chin. 'I'm a little reluctant to verbalise my D-E-S-I-R-E, as Ester might say. I'll wait until you read out yours, Ester'.

'All right, Bonnie, but there's no need to hold back. The three of us have kept the wishes our secret since the beginning'. Ester looks at her page. 'I've progressed a little since last year. My number one last year was like Hilda's; health and fitness. Thanks to my tennis partners for that. My second one was joy in my life'.

'Mother of God', says Hilda. 'How do you parse that one?'

'Sex, Hilda. Pleasure. Desire. Call it what you like, that act of passion. Oh, I don't know what I'm talking about'.

There is silence again. The room is trapped in time. The women are winding back the years.

Bonnie looks at the two women. 'It goes on until the grave'.

'What does?' Hilda's eyes light up.

'Desire, Hilda'. Bonnie plays with the word, opens her mouth as if she is tasting the sounds for the first time; the same way Ester did earlier.

'Bonnie, we've yet to hear of your third wish', says Ester. 'Come on, out with it'.

'Right, but promise not to laugh', Bonnie pleads. 'Since we're all being honest about our desires, I'll put mine on the record. I would love Nigella Lawson to bring me breakfast in bed and then to join me under the duvet for a cup of tea. Just for once in my life. Now it's out. I've said it'.

Hilda puts her hand on Bonnie's shoulder. 'We can arrange that, love'.

Ester smiles. 'My third wish last year will be the same for next year and that is that we meet again with joy in our hearts'.

The wishes are made now; in fact, remade. They are almost a repeat of the ones of the previous year. The papers are sellotaped on the back of Bonnie's aunt and uncle and the portrait reinstated for another year. With business completed, Ester and Hilda say their goodbyes. They leave the apartment; facing the dark of the night. Two bookends with the coming year's wishes between them.

Bonnie pulls over a kitchen chair to the window to see her friends' departure. She waves regally to them as their car drifts away out of sight. What a lovely night it is out there, she thinks, and what a lovely evening in here. She looks up at the full moon through her dark glasses.

How could anyone believe that there was a man in the moon? To her, the moon has always been much more a feminine force. She searches the sky for stars, but the moon is the centre of the constellation, the leading light.

Hello, my beautiful moon.

Giddiness takes hold of her and she sings out.

'I see the moon, the moon sees me'.

Clapping her hands together, she applauds the yellow orb. She turns to make her way back to the kitchen. She has forgotten that she is standing on a chair. Her little body crumples to the floor.

Bonnie wakes up in hospital. Both her wrists are broken but this fact pales into insignificance when she sees the nurse looking down at her.

'Nigella!'

Her gentle brown eyes soft and her heaving breasts covered in white satin.

'I'll have to feed you breakfast, Bonnie', the young nurse's assistant says.

Bonnie smiles at her.

'Thank you, Nigella. You are so good'.

She inhales deeply and closes her eyes.

The curtains in Bonnie's living room are drawn and the air is dank.

'Let in some light, Ester, and give the room a bit of fresh air'.

They both sit down in silence, taking in the familiar surroundings and breathing in the swirling memories it holds, now mixed with the freshening breeze from the sea.

'Let's put the kettle on before we do anything'.

Ester goes into the kitchen and Hilda follows. Ester lights the gas. While blowing out the match, she notices a photo of Bonnie, hidden behind the tea caddy.

'She mustn't have wanted anyone to see this', Ester hands the photo to Hilda.

'God love her, would you look at the hump on her back. I wonder who took that one; you can bet your life on it she didn't know she was being captured on her bad side'.

Bonnie's hump was something that no one had ever discussed; not in the office, nor at the theatre, not even among her friends. It was always a question mark unanswered.

The two women set the tray and take their tea to the sitting room.

'Here's to Bonnie'. They clink their cups together.

'Read out that letter again, Ester'.

The Last Will and Testament of Bonnie O'Rourke

In the matter of my personal effects, I wish that my two best friends, Ester O'Connell and Hilda Kelly-Brown, take possession of my diary for their own private reading and also that they have first choice from my library of books and pictures.

Both women know about Bonnie's diary; it was always kept in the same place, on the low table, but never opened, not even in their presence. Ester picks up the green leather-bound book and holds it tenderly between her hands, as if it were a fragile baby.

'Somebody once said that the next biggest sin after murder was reading someone else's diary'.

Hilda smiles at her friend.

'She wants us to have it. There'll be nothing in it except her reviews of plays and concerts, and goodness knows we've heard enough about those over the years'.

'What about Nuala?'

'Oh, no, Ester. Don't ...'

But Ester has already opened the book, splaying her fingers to ensure none of the many loose paper cuttings and cards fall to the floor. The first entry concerns a Wagner concert at the National Concert Hall, dated 11 November 1993. The comment under the review is:

Music too dramatic for my taste. I think Mr Wagner was a bit of a show off, but I have to admit I like the style of his personal dress. The programme note referred to the fact that when he was composing his music he insisted on dressing up and used to declare to his friends that he only wanted to be surrounded by beauty. In that department, Mr Wagner, we have something in common.

Hilda sighs. 'Poor Bonnie. We were so used to her theatrical costumes. Do you remember the pom-poms?'

Ester turns the well-read pages filled with years of quiet drama. The account of plays comes to an end at the point where Bonnie had suffered her stroke, at the age of eighty-one. After that, the nature of the entries changes. The next few pages have cards glued neatly into the folds of the book. What surprises Ester most of all is seeing a card that she herself had sent to Bonnie when she was away on one of her tennis weekends. The colours now faded, it has the figures of two tennis players on the cover. The message inside reads: *I am a bit late in discovering tennis, Bonnie, but it has given me new energy. Will tell you all when I see you. Your dear friend, Ester.*

Bonnie's comment on the next page reads: *Hmm. Must ask Ester what she means by 'new energy'?*

'Mother of God, Ester, have a heart. She was in her eighties!'

Then Hilda spots a photo of her sons, Paul and James, with Bonnie. The photo is pasted under James' birthday. Bonnie smiles out proudly from between the two boys. She had written over the photo: *My two best boyfriends.*

'You have something to show for your years, Hilda'.

Hilda stares at the photo. 'What good are my sons to me now, Ester, tell me that? Their wives have taken them. Bonnie used to say that men were messy, but children are messy as well. Do you know something, Ester? Men come and go, but women are with you forever. It is only in friendship we can be ourselves'. Hilda is surprised by the depth of her own feelings. But she is on a roll now and can't stop herself. 'You were as well off, Ester, without children. I know you wasted too much of your child-bearing years on that loser, but it was the best day of your life when you finished with him ...'

Ester is not listening. Hilda bites her lip. 'Right. Which of us will keep custody of the diary?'

Ester doesn't want to close the book abruptly. She gently turns the pages. The next section is headed TELEVISION. She reads aloud one of Bonnie's final entries:

The only good thing about television is that I can turn down the sound and feel that I have company in the room. The soaps are so unappealing, nobody seems to be able to either act or speak, and they all seem to have the same storyline. Last Saturday I watched a chat show hosted by a very charming good-looking young woman, but she could only ask the women guests about their children and their marital status. Does she not think there is more to women than marriage and children? These days I only look at one programme, the cookery one.

Below this entry is written, in big block capitals:

IS THERE NOT A WORLD ELSEWHERE? HORATIO, HORATIO, WHEREFORE, ART THOU?

Hilda sighs. 'She was beginning to lose it then'.

Ester has a final quick look through the diary. 'No sign of Nuala. I wonder was she a figment of her imagination?' She stands. 'There's just one thing left, Hilda, that we must carry out of here together'.

Ester takes down the portrait of Bonnie's aunt and uncle from over the mantlepiece. Hiding behind the picture are the secret wishes of the three women.

They walk along Dún Laoghaire pier. The pale blue of the sky merges with the sea, casting a gentle light on the harbour.

'She went so fast, poor Bonnie'. Hilda is surprised to find that she is near tears. 'You know, I swear to God, she believed that Nigella was catering to her every need up until the end'.

'Her every need?' Ester ponders over these little words. 'None of us know what our every need is. Certainly I don't think Bonnie did'.

'I wouldn't be too sure about that, Ester. She knew she was never interested in men'.

The two women have reached the end of the pier. They look out to sea.

'Does this mean there will be no more wishes next year, Ester? We can hardly make them without Bonnie'.

'True, but the tide isn't going to stop coming in and out because Bonnie is dead. What is your every need, Hilda?'

'Will you stop going on about that, Ester, and grow up'. Hilda is becoming annoyed. She looks around, making sure nobody is listening. Then she notices the tears in her friend's eyes. The tide of hope is fast running out in Ester's heart. Hilda thinks of Bonnie's words.

'You're not dead yet, Ester'.

She links her friend's arm. And the tide rises and they walk on together.

OFFENDERS

Daphne sat upright in her seat, listening to the words coming out of the thin mouth of the man behind the podium.

> *There are huge areas of the human condition that we cannot readily explain, despite recent success stories in medical and neuroscience. Emotions, the field of sexual feelings. It is a fact that we know more about outer space than we do about the inner space of our emotional world ...*

She looked around at the fifty or so delegates in the conference room of Hunter's Hotel. It was the opening address of the weekend symposium and Daphne was the designated teacher from her prison. The background of the other people in the audience was unknown to her, but she understood that all worked in the field of sexual deviancy. The speaker was Dr Edward Golden from London.

Daphne worked as a drama teacher in a small prison in the Irish midlands where the majority of the inmates were sex offenders. The delegates were now giving Dr Golden a standing ovation, but Daphne remained seated. There was nothing new to her in what he said. She wondered was she being churlish. Looking around, she saw a man smile at her. He had also remained seated.

It was late afternoon and the May evening was stretching out ahead. Dinner at seven. It was Daphne's first visit to the hotel, so she decided to wander around the grounds. A walk would clear her head. The grass stretched down in a slope at the back. She hadn't realised that the hotel was on a hill. When she'd arrived by taxi earlier in the day, her mind had been elsewhere.

A circle of cherry blossom trees drew her down to a small garden. She sat on the seat and closed her eyes. Her husband's voice screamed in her ears.

'You're never here when you're needed, what sort of a mother are you?'

She hated when he raised his voice.

She knew what sort of a mother she was; a very bad one. He would never forgive her the many misdemeanours in their marriage, but her most recent offence was not being present at their son's first communion two months ago. Their son didn't seem to mind. He was used to his mother's bouts of depression. He called them 'mammy's little episodes', a phrase he had learned from his father.

There is nothing more beautiful than cherry blossoms. They reminded her of her wedding day; a day like today, balmy and bright, a day full of hope for the future, a day that had held such promise nearly a decade ago.

It was Friday evening now and she was missing the visit to the pub with her colleagues. It was a tradition that, at the end of the working week, a group of teachers would congregate in the local pub. There was always bound to be someone Daphne knew, and very often she would go there alone and sit among the group, listening to the stories of the week. Sometimes she would arrive home late and find her husband in bed and the odd time she wouldn't come home at all until the next day.

This Friday, she'd been given the day off to attend the seminar. Time to herself was what she wanted, time to think. She studied the programme for the two days. Dinner tonight and workshops in the morning after breakfast.

On her way up to her room she stopped outside the dining-hall to read the notice of the table layout for the evening. Seeing her name there mingled with those of delegates from other countries gave her a certain sense of importance. It had only been two years since she had been offered a full-time position in the prison system. She didn't feel that she had enough experience to be partaking in such a conference, but she hoped that she might learn a thing or two. Her name was between a Dr Marie-Pierre Fisher from France and a Dr Marcus Webster from Belfast.

They were already seated at the table when she arrived. Marie-Pierre Fisher was a woman in her fifties, a psychologist who had recently taken up an appointment in a women's prison outside of Paris.

'The majority of the women prisoners are drug addicts. What I'm discovering is that more than half of them are victims of sexual abuse in childhood'.

Daphne was looking forward to eating the boeuf bourguignone that had been placed in front of her and did not feel like engaging in any topic that related to work. There was all of tomorrow for such dialogue. Marcus Webster, on the other side of her, was chewing on his goujons of sole.

'Beautiful', he smiled at her. 'How is yours?'

It was only when he smiled that she realised he was the man she had seen earlier, the one like her who had remained seated, who hadn't stood up to applaud at the opening address by Dr Golden. The waiter poured wine and left two bottles, one white and one red.

'A very generous menu. I'm not sure who funds these events. Have you any idea?'

Marcus Webster was looking at Daphne. He had a very sensuous mouth. She guessed he wasn't yet forty.

'As far as I know, a number of sources fund this sort of thing. From the north and the south'.

She wasn't sure, so she changed the subject.

'What part of the country are you working in?'

He hesitated before answering. She thought she noticed a faint pink glow cover his face.

'I'm not sure, really. I'm waiting to be appointed to two different prisons in Northern Ireland. Perhaps I shouldn't really be here, but my bishop thought it would be beneficial for me to attend in some capacity'.

Daphne didn't know what way to take this explanation. It wasn't fair, she thought, that a man should exude such sex appeal and then declare his neutrality. It was easy to hide behind one's profession. She changed the subject.

'I work in the south. I'm a drama teacher in a male prison where the majority of the inmates are sex offenders'.

'A drama teacher. I love theatre', he said, and filled up her glass and then his own.

Daphne's room was next to Marie-Pierre Fisher's. They both took the lift to the third floor. Marcus remained on. 'I'm one up on you', he said as he pointed upwards.

The wine had gone to Daphne's head. She felt elated, almost happy. The bedroom overlooked the back of the hotel and she could see the cherry blossom trees and the circle of seats where she had sat earlier in the evening. Already she was looking forward to the next session in the morning and meeting Marcus again. A little indulgence was called for. A bath would be the luxury she needed. She filled the tub and poured in a lavish amount of seaweed & arnica infusion. On the label of the bottle was written: *A Restorative Bath to Enjoy when Overtired.*

Stretched out in the bath she examined her body and thought – not at all bad for forty. It had been a long time since her husband had commented on her body and even longer since he had touched her. She remembered the day that the cracks had started to appear between them. After three years of her failure to become pregnant, they had decided to investigate the reasons and the tests had revealed an unusually low sperm count. It was the beginning of the downward slope. Low everything after that, low sex drive, and low self-esteem, until she finally came up with a solution.

The early morning sun streamed in through the crack in the curtains and Daphne decided to get up. After a shower, she took more than her usual time deciding what outfit to wear. Two items of clothing were hanging side by side in her wardrobe. The new Top Shop blue jeans were competing with the black Marks and Spencer's dress, her husband's present for her fortieth birthday a few weeks earlier. Marcus's sensuous mouth came into her head and she could see again the slow movements of his lips as he ate his meal. She pulled the jeans on and had to lie on the bed to pull up the zip. They fitted like another layer of skin. A white silk blouse with pearl buttons completed the outfit. She left the top button open and was pleased with her reflection in the long mirror, so pleased she smiled and said it out loud.

'You're not all bad, kid'.

The knock on her door brought her back to earth. It was Marie-Pierre.

'Are you coming down for breakfast?'

When they arrived at the same table as the night before, the waitress took their orders. There was no sign of Marcus; his place name had disappeared.

A choice of two morning workshops: one on 'group management', mainly aimed towards teachers, and the other on 'therapeutic practice and the sexual deviant'. Daphne parted company with Marie-Pierre and went into the room for teachers. The chairs were arranged in a circle. Only two of them were still empty. It was not yet ten o'clock. Daphne was impressed by the punctuality of the other delegates. At a minute before ten, Marcus arrived and sat in the remaining empty chair beside Daphne.

'Did you skip breakfast?' The question was out of her mouth before she realised it might have been too intrusive.

'No, I had an early breakfast. I had a little more preparation to do for this session'.

She didn't realise any preparation was necessary. Then the penny dropped.

'Good morning, everyone. I'm Marcus Webster and I'm your facilitator for this session. May I start by introducing myself? Then I'll continue the introductions around the circle, beginning with Daphne here on my left. My background is in psychoanalysis and my work up until now has been in mental institutions, working with groups of recovering patients. After our introductions I will divide you into smaller teams with specific tasks which I will explain later. Teamwork will be at the heart of the work we do today. As you all are aware, teamwork is bigger than the sum of its parts ...'

He was brief, but he'd left the group in no doubt as to his credentials. Daphne admired that; she had always found talking about herself very difficult. It sprang from a childhood belief that talking about yourself was boastful, lacking in good manners.

'I've been working with sex offenders in a prison context for the past two years', she said. 'My subject area is drama'.

Marcus, of course, knew this from their conversation the previous night; but that Marcus was not the same as the man now listening to her. This man was businesslike, almost cold.

'Thank you, Daphne. Do you mind sharing with the group what your qualifications are and what training you underwent to prepare for such work?'

She felt she was on trial and was a little taken aback. It was a long time since anyone had asked her questions about her work qualifications. To her surprise she heard herself speaking in her 'sexy' voice, the one she used to use when she was chatting up her colleagues in the pub on a Friday night.

'No, I don't mind sharing at all. Isn't that the reason we are all here? Some years ago, I did a masters degree in England in drama therapy in education and discovered that it worked well in my present field of work ...'

Marcus continued around the group, extracting the precise nature of their work and their qualifications. He then arranged the participants into smaller numbers of four and allotted them one hour to discuss the personality make-up of the typical group of offenders. After making sure that the task was clear, he left the room.

By now, Daphne was listening to teachers who knew their clients and she felt she had a lot in common with them. At eleven on the dot, Marcus returned. He announced that after a coffee break he would chair a feedback session and explore methods of techniques and strategies in the field of work with sex offenders.

After coffee, the workshop resumed with Marcus at the helm. He stood at the top of the room in front of a flipchart, armed with a packet of multi-coloured pens. The circle opened up and Marcus asked Daphne's group to select one major area of difficulty. She was the elected spokesperson. The group consensus was that the field of incest was the most difficult and complex area of their work. Marcus asked what gender the offenders were. 'Male, of course'. Daphne regretted her tone immediately. Yet why should she? The gender of the offender in the morning's discussion had been exclusively male. Female sex offenders were not on the agenda.

Marcus looked at Daphne and she could feel the colour rising in her cheeks. Without any warning, another image of Marcus had crept into her mind. She was visualising him in another setting. In her head she was playing out a drama of being a sex offender and choreographing how and where she might target Marcus.

'Does the neuropsychology of sex differ between men and women?' she found herself asking. She knew that her question wasn't really about her work. Damn it all, but it wasn't only men that had sexual urges and needs. If a woman was in a marriage without sex, why shouldn't she seek it elsewhere? Marriage wasn't meant to be a prison. It might be acceptable for priests and nuns to take the vow of celibacy, but it wasn't what she had signed up for when she married.

The room of eyes focussed on her. A long pause stretched between Marcus and herself. There was no point attending these seminars if she couldn't get something out of them for herself. Marcus opened up her question to the group. One of the two other men stuttered.

'Men are programmed to have sex with as many partners as possible'.

That old chestnut, Daphne thought. She couldn't stop herself.

'Is that because women are programmed to have kids? Are you saying our maternal nature negates our sex drive?'

'We are still learning about the neuropsychology of sex', Marcus intervened.

Daphne looked at her watch. She was relieved to see it was nearly lunchtime.

Marie-Pierre had arrived at the table before her. The waiter served the soup. Daphne hoped Marie-Pierre would be staying for dinner in the evening. She was beginning to warm to this woman; she felt she could tell her anything or ask her anything. But she wouldn't; some things are best kept to yourself.

'Was there anything of interest in your group?'

Marie-Pierre smiled and Daphne wondered if she was referring to Marcus. He was seated at another table now, with Dr Golden and the invited panel for the plenary session in the afternoon. She realised why he had not been present at her table since the opening night. He was in a different league to her. Daphne explained to Marie-Pierre how uneasy she had felt about the morning's session.

'I feel that I let myself down by becoming emotional. I shouldn't have brought my own personal feelings into a discussion on male deviancy'.

'Why not, Daphne? Are we females all that different to men?' Marie-Pierre looked at Daphne thoughtfully. 'Maybe you need to challenge your facilitator to look beyond his male prejudices'.

After lunch, Daphne checked to see if there was anybody from the conference at the reception desk. As soon as the coast was clear, she asked for the number of Marcus's room. She knew it was a bad idea but some fierce compulsion was driving her. She went up to her own room first. His room number – room 413, fourth floor – was etched in her head. Should she call in on him now? Show him what was what, loosen him up, or wait till later in the day? She sat on the edge of her bed and sprayed on her favourite Noir perfume. All the men she'd had sex with in the early days of her marriage flashed by her. They were easy prey. But desire wasn't what had fuelled the sex, it had been something else. After a few minutes she made up her mind. She would write him a letter.

> Dear Marcus,
> Can we meet in the cherry blossom garden after the plenary session?
> I have some questions about the afternoon workshop.
> Daphne.

She looked at the letter in her hand. No time like the present. She took the lift up to the fourth floor and walked towards room 413. The door was open and a chambermaid was undressing the bed. Daphne walked into the room and asked where Marcus was.

'He will be collecting his suitcase and other belongings. He is leaving today'.

The girl moved Marcus's suitcase and the wardrobe door swung open. A white robe was hanging inside. When Daphne saw it, she was stuck to the spot. The white of the robe brought back the white jacket that she had bought for her son's first communion. The day she had been absent from. The innocent face of her son, smiling at her.

All that day she had stayed in her bed, crying.

'The age of reason is where we're supposed to be'.

Her husband kept repeating the phrase: 'the age of reason, the bloody age of reason'.

Daphne had chosen the evening before the communion day to be honest with him. She had told him that she had slept with other men to become pregnant, but that she was sure that he was the real father of the child.

'Of all the times in the world to tell me, you chose the night before our son's special day'.

He told her that he couldn't bear to look at her. She had decided that the best course of action was to stay away from the ceremony.

She left the room, the letter still in her hand. Her heart was thumping and the floodgates had opened; tears were streaming down her face. As she hurried back towards the lift, she saw Marcus. He was making his way towards her.

'Oh, Daphne. I hope you enjoy the afternoon session. I'm really sorry to be missing it. Some urgent business to attend to at the monastery'.

He held his hand out to her. She struggled to find something to say. What she really wanted from him was forgiveness, absolution. She was losing the run of herself.

'I hope we meet again, Marcus, and good luck with your work'.

Marcus was a good man. It was she who was the deviant; she had been carrying the guilt of not knowing who the father of her child was for all the years of the boy's lifetime. She knew she had to rid herself of the guilt, but not like this.

The afternoon session with the entire group of delegates went smoothly and predictable. Proposals were debated and agreed. The statement from Daphne's group was that a multidisciplinary approach was good in itself, but it required teamwork to succeed. Daphne was strangely pleased about the inclusion of the teamwork element in the statement. Hearing it read aloud she thought, isn't all of life about teamwork? Doesn't it exist at every level? Then it struck her, like a bell ringing in her head, that teamwork was not at the heart of her life, not between herself and her husband. There was something broken at the core of her marriage. A decision crystallised in her mind. She would phone her husband later and ask him to meet her at the train station. The delegates' dinner that she had been so looking forward to held no attraction for her now.

Marie-Pierre was sorry to hear that she had to go home urgently and hoped that everything would work out for her.

'Daphne, one of the delegates from your group was telling me how successful your drama therapy was in your work. I'd love to hear more. Can I give you my card and perhaps we can meet soon?'

The train journey back felt like she was returning from a foreign place where she had learned a new language. She would tell her husband all about it. She would seek his forgiveness. It was also clear to her that she was due an element of forgiveness from him if they were to continue. The train stopped at its final destination and she saw her husband and son on the platform, waiting for her. The boy stood close to his father. Like a young branch, thought Daphne, that had been successfully grafted onto the mature solid trunk of a well-rooted tree.

LANDLOCKED

Finn decided his next big purchase would be a camera.
The changing colours outside his kitchen window were
worth recording. It would be another source of occupation.
It didn't bother him that his house stood alone, a wide gap
separating him from his neighbours. It was that wide gap
that would prove the subject matter for his new camera.
Those changing hues of yellow, orange and purple. Grey
boulders cooled down the boastful gorse, heather and
montbretia. Every morning at this time he studied the
view before his breakfast. The lone birch tree at the end of
his garden held his attention. He studied a large magpie
that had perched on the highest branch, observing that the
branch held the bird without a quiver. It remained as still
as the standing erratic boulders in the next field. The front
of the house faced the main road between the village on
one side and the road stretching towards the sea on the
other. This was his world now.

The phone ringing startled him. The cup of tea in his right hand splashed over his white T-shirt. Finn swivelled his chair, screeching the wheels towards his landline.

'We've found someone for you'.

Social Welfare had promised a new home-help. The previous one, a middle-aged woman had walked out on him more than two weeks before. The locals in this tiny community on the edge of the Atlantic had avoided such work. Were they afraid of what the neighbours might think? Two years had slowly passed since his arrival in this haunted place but Finn had had his reasons for setting up house here.

'She's from Prague and speaks perfect English', Mary said.

'That makes a change from the last one. She refused to speak any English'.

'That's the way it is here'. Mary was using her bossy voice. A position in the Social Welfare office gave authority to the employees. Blow-ins, like Finn, needed to be taught the local facts of life.

'This is a Gaeltacht area, sir. It's important we hold on to our first language'.

Finn knew it was more to do with economics. The Irish language spoke when the government grants were being doled out. But he was well rid of the last home-help. It galled him to think of her gloating about his past with the women at the shops.

'The new girl will call on Monday. It will be a trial period for both of you', Mary said, as she hung up. We'll wait and see, thought Finn.

A wave of calm soothed his nerves, probably something to do with the thought of meeting a real human being. It seemed like a lifetime ago since he had properly spoken to another soul, face to face.

It was Saturday – his favourite evening for television. Weekends for Finn only meant one thing and that was his dance programme. The 9 o'clock news and *Strictly Come Dancing* were the only programmes he watched. Radio was his preferred choice of distraction and sometimes when he was in a good mood he might listen to one of his CDs. Both dance music. Both waltz collections. An obsession with ballroom dancing had set him apart from his peers from an early age. There was something in his make-up that responded to the music of the waltz. The *da, da, da, da, da, di, dum, di, dum* penetrated a depth that he couldn't understand. The gym teacher from his secondary school had introduced him to ballroom dancing classes where eventually he progressed to competitions on a national level. Aged twelve he represented Ireland in Brighton. Looking back at his life now it shocked him to think it had been the only time he had travelled outside the country. Brighton, on the south coast of England. To-night's *Strictly* was taking place in the Brighton Dome. Finn knew the beach there from his young dancing competition days.

This morning there was nothing in his cupboard to eat except for the last tin of something or other. He would skip breakfast again today.

The small house was wheelchair friendly. It was almost like the wheels of his chair knew the map of the house and all the corners to avoid. Renovations had been carried out for a previous tenant, now deceased. Finn was fortunate that the vacancy had occurred during his release from prison two summers ago. A new energy ran through him now after that phone call. He examined his empty cupboard again, one tin of tuna to be precise. He knew what he had to do.

The back garden was Finn's only exit point to the world. A small space of land, covered now with neat rows of carrots, potatoes and spinach. Beyond the back wall a hillside opened to golden gorse bushes and big grey boulders and, in the summertime, heather and montbretia.

Needs must, thought Finn, and he set himself to the task of digging. The handle of the spade was just the right length for him. He had mastered the technique of digging by leaning his body weight against the handle. A strong leather strap secured his hips to the chair. During the activity he sang the phrases of the *Strictly* judges in time with each 'rise and fall' of the spade. *Da, da, da, da*. Digging into the earth was another form of upper body exercise. Gently placing the carrots, onions, spinach and potatoes into the satchel at the back of his chair, he glided back to his kitchen. The world was looking better now, sun lifting the sky and his mood rising. He would prepare for the rest of the day starting with his shower.

He changed his tea stained T-shirt and set about his physical work-out, stretching both arms and raising them towards the ceiling. A ritual practice after the garden exertions; criss-crossing them in a circle, before bringing them down to rest on his thighs. If only his legs would obey his commands in the same way.

Tonight, the final episode of *Strictly Come Dancing* and Finn's excitement was beginning to creep up on him. He was feeling giddy as if he were expecting a visitor to his house. Nobody ever visited. Except, of course, the home-help. He mustn't think of that, not for the moment anyway. Meditation was what he needed to practice now.

Seven years in prison had taught him very little. Meditation was the only useful skill that he had come out into the world with and, of course, his dead legs. 'Conversion Hysteria' they had called his condition. A psychologist had told him that Freud had named it thus and it was related to an imagined trauma. There was nothing imagined about Finn's trauma.

During the last few months he had found meditation a sort of comfort. It wasn't every day that he would practice but today he would apply himself to a thirty minute session before his lunch. It was another means of passing the day, at least part of it. Time to think, but the whole philosophy of meditation was to still the body and mind, providing a pause in his day so that he could take stock of where he was.

The carrots and onions from the morning's dig would make a light soup, take the edge off his hunger. Later in the afternoon he would scrub and scrape the spuds, rinse the spinach and open his last tin of tuna so that his stomach wouldn't grumble while he watched and entered into the world of his favourite programme.

He dreamt during the night that he was waltzing across an empty ballroom floor, his shoulders back and down and his feet pointed at exactly the right angle that the judges on telly had indicated. He had his left hand around a tiny waist but he couldn't see the girl's face. The sensation of heat at the closeness of her body remained with him after waking. He thought he could feel a tingling spasm in his right foot as he eased himself into his wheelchair. Len's words were in his head when he lifted his two feet onto the step of the chair.

'Dancing is all about the feet, it's all about footwork'.

Da, da, da, da, da, di, dum ...

It was 10am when the doorbell rang. Sunday. Nobody ever rang on his door, especially not on a Sunday and it took him some time to decide whether to answer it or not. He lifted the hand-set of the intercom on the wall.

'Who is it?'

'It's Katya, your new home-help, sir'.

She entered his house and he was lost for words. The girl reminded him of someone he had liked during his teacher training days in the Gaeltacht, those days that were to qualify him as a permanent pensionable teacher, a job for life. She had the same red hair, open smile and big brown eyes. The only difference was that her hair was cut very short and she reminded him of Sinead O'Connor.

'I'm Katya', she said again and went to shake his hand. 'Mary said that you would tell me about my duties'.

The girl was keen, she was a day early. Finn couldn't decide what way he felt: on the one hand, he didn't like surprises like this, but on the other, he was disorientated by the girl's warm smile. It took him a while to compose himself. Finally, he made the decision to welcome her.

'Please take your coat off and sit down'.

Katya wasn't wearing a coat, but it was a phrase of welcome that was ingrained in him. The first invitation his mother had suggested to any visitor entering her house was to take off their coats and make themselves comfortable. He could hear his mother's voice: 'I didn't even ask them to take their coats off when they arrived at my door'. His mind flashed back to the period before his arrest. Seven years ago now. Was it the seven year itch that brought him to a place like this? An itch that had to be scratched.

The whiteness of Katya's blouse reminded him now of his childhood innocence. It had a calming effect on his nervous stomach. The brightness of her presence at his solitary table pleased his aesthetic sense. She wasn't like that slovenly woman from the islands, who had shuffled her feet and scratched her head while he was giving her his grocery list. God knows, that was all he had asked the woman to do.

'I can do most things myself', he said. 'But I need a few errands from the village every so often'.

'Do you want me to do any housework?'

Finn was independent to a fault, despite the fact that he had been institutionalised for those seven years in prison. Now, he struggled hard to remain self-sufficient. Every new step in his routine caused him sleepless nights until he learned to cope with the changes.

'Ar mhaith leat cupán tae?'

It was Finn's attempt to be friendly; he didn't want to scare this one away. But her eyes narrowed and he realised that she couldn't possibly understand Irish. He tried again, this time in English.

'Would you like a cup of tea?' He looked at her again.

A smile of amusement lit across her young face.

'Oh, yes, but let me make it, please'.

She made her way towards the sink. The kettle was placed beside the low taps. She looked around for his permission. He nodded and she bent down to fill it. Everything in the kitchen was designed to satisfy Finn's wheelchair height. He watched her movements. Try as he might, he couldn't stop himself from being excited by the shape of her blue-jeaned hips as she extended over the sink, her long legs straightening again as she filled the kettle. Finn had never had any real relationships with women, only crushes that played out in his dreams.

Katya placed two chipped cups on the table and looked at Finn. He let out a little cough, in an attempt to cover his red face with his big hands. He watched her glide over to the fridge to get the milk. The thought of her seeing his empty shelves embarrassed him. He was in denial, even to himself, that he was helpless when it came to items that were needed from the village shop. Now, at this very moment, whilst watching Katya move around in his kitchen, it dawned on him that he was not as independent as he pretended. He would learn to be a little more open with her, that is, if she stayed with him. He could hear himself thinking about her departure and was already consoling himself in preparation for it. They drank their tea in silence. His eyes were fixed on her hands. Every movement was gentle and slow. The steady way she led the spoon around the cup almost hypnotised him. Oh God, was he getting ahead of himself?

'Please say again the Irish for cup of tea?'

Her lips opened and her wide eyes focused on his mouth as he slowly pronounced 'cupán tae'. It was agreed between them that she would call the next day at 10am and he would have a list of errands drawn up for her. Finn left the girl to the door and watched after her as she disappeared down his small front path and down the road towards the village.

Of course, he had forgotten to ask her where she lived, what had brought her to Ireland and more to the point what was she doing in a small Irish-speaking village on the west coast. The only thing he knew about her was her name – Katya. A name similar to Kathleen, or in these parts, Cáit. There was only one woman that came to mind with that name that had made an impact on his life and that was the cruel woman who had taught his group Irish. Cáit got the job that year, teaching the blow-ins what they should have been taught in their primary schools. She had hurled abuse at the class, many of whom were qualified art and literacy teachers and were too afraid to complain about her for fear of failing the exam and losing a career in the teaching profession.

A crescendo of voices from the opposite direction of the village sent Finn back indoors. It was the last week of the summer school. The teenagers passed by his house at this time every day on their way back to their Mná Tí for lunch. He didn't want to hear the comments that he thought they might make. Once had been enough for him.

'There lives the man who murdered his teacher'.

He would never forget his past and neither would this village allow him to.

Sunrise came early. It seemed to Finn that since Katya arrived it came earlier every morning but, of course, he knew it was the natural progression of the summer season. It had been exactly this day four weeks ago that she had first knocked on his door. He was counting his blessings. Even the bathroom showed signs of change. Each time she shopped she had brought back extra items that were not on his list. Hand towels with a rainbow stripe on the edges, two for the price of one. Two china mugs from token stamps collected over her first two weeks. She had brought more than a hint of elegance into his world. Yesterday she had told him that she was learning Irish in the community centre and had asked him if he would help her with homework.

A Nikon camera was draped around her neck and Finn thought she looked different.

'It's too hot for indoors this morning, Finn. Would you like to go for a walk to the Yellow Strand?'

She might as well have asked him did he want to fly to the moon. Places outside his hall door were foreign territory to him. This August would mark the second year of his life in this house and up until now his boundaries of movement had ranged from his garden at the back to the door at the front. Television and radio were his links to the outside world and work on his movements started with *Strictly*. He was in control of his world and he didn't want anyone to interfere.

'No, I wouldn't'.

He pushed his wheels away from her and looked out at his garden. All he could see now were the weeds growing between his vegetable drills. Katya filled the silence with making herself busy.

The audacity of the woman, thinking she can wheel me out for all the world to mock. The idea of it stuck in his throat. He could feel his blood rising.

'Katya, it's time that you and I had a talk'.

In her hands were the folded sheets she had finished ironing even though Finn had told her there was no need to iron his bedclothes. The woman was getting too close – but he couldn't bear the thought of her leaving him, not now, not when he couldn't do without her. Turning away from her, he jerked his wheelchair towards the worktop to put the kettle on. She immediately read the action.

'Ar mhaith leat cupán tae?'

As she placed the two new china cups on the table, she said, 'I feel at home in the Irish language. I think it must have been my native tongue in a previous existence'.

Finn couldn't stop a smile. He was reminded of a similar conversation with the girl he had met during his time in the Gaeltacht all those years ago. He had been too shy to communicate his feelings then. Try as he might he couldn't even remember her name now. They were both sitting on a big rock at the edge of the sea. She had said something about being at peace in the presence of the Irish language, there was something about the rhythm of the speech, the sounds of the words that penetrated the bloodstream. It was a rhythm in tune with the tides of the sea. Finn had agreed with her, he felt the very same way, the same inexplicable pull towards this place.

'Yes, you're definitely improving, you're an excellent student', he told Katya.

A big smile from her then showed off her perfect gleaming teeth.

'What are you doing with that camera?'

'My mother sent it to me for my thirtieth birthday'.

Finn was surprised to hear that she was already thirty, only a year younger than himself.

'The sea is all around us here, Finn, and I want to send some photos home to the Czech Republic'.

'Why?'

'My daughter adores the sea. I want her to come here, Finn. To this magical place. In our country we have no sea'.

'You're landlocked?'

Finn surprised himself with this phrase. It had never occurred to him before that anyone could miss the sea. He had always taken it for granted. Here, all roads led to the sea. Indeed, all his life he had lived near the sea. The family home in Clontarf was on the seafront. As a child he had played there with his brother and friends. He had to admit that during his incarceration he hadn't given the sea a single thought and that had surprised him most of all. He wasn't himself during those years of displacement. His mother's visits became unbearable, her sympathy was a huge source of annoyance and eventually he told her he didn't want to see her or his brother again. He had told them to forget about him.

'Do you know, Finn, that I speak to the cashier in the supermarket now *as Gaeilge*'.

He was gob-smacked. She was only a few weeks in the place and was nearly talking like a local.

'The girl in the shop told me that if I lived here for another few months I could put my name down on the Housing List'.

His thoughts were in turmoil now and he knew he had to take time to let them sift through the storm in his head. There was something not quite right here, the events were moving too fast.

'Will I pour the tea now?'

He looked at her smooth and capable hands as she lifted the teapot and he wanted to take hold of them. He watched the dance of her movements as she stirred the spoon around the cup, placing it back on its saucer, lifting the cup to her mouth. Her presence in his life was so smooth and comfortable, he didn't want anything to interrupt it. She reminded him of the bird on the birch; she was part of his life now and her presence flowed without touching a nerve. At least, that is, up until today. Seeing her every day in his domain was one thing. He knew where she was and knew every movement of the day but her wanting to take him out of his own house had been a step too far.

'Katya, there is something I have to tell you'.

A smile – this time across her eyes and then she whispered.

'I know, Finn. You pushed your teacher. Everyone knows it was an accident and that you were only protecting yourself from her anger. The whole village knows you were so badly punished for something that wasn't your fault'. She looked straight at him before continuing. 'Did you know, Finn, that is why you got your house? People here wanted to make amends to you'. Katya took a deep breath and became very serious. 'That woman, Cáit, that teacher, was a bully who thought teachers who weren't fluent in the Irish language were traitors and needed to be punished. She was sick. The women have told me many times about her and how she was allowed to teach without any qualifications. They told me that her father was the brother of the parish priest'.

Finn couldn't decide whether she meant these comments or whether she was playing him for a fool. Had she been talking about him to the women in the shops? Was she, after all, just like the woman from the islands? He had never asked her why she had come to this part of the world.

He didn't feel like revealing his life story to her now. The facts were on record.

'A young student strikes his teacher a brutal blow, sentencing her to life in a coma'.

It was so long ago, but the consequences lived on with him every day of his life. A year after the accident, Cáit had been declared dead and her family issued murder proceedings against Finn. The event had brought his teaching ambition to an end. He had left prison after seven years with not a penny in his pocket and his prospects ruined. The death of his mother the year before Finn was released had been another blow to him. She had left the family home to his younger brother, cutting him out of his inheritance. The Irish language he had told himself owed him something and he would find a way to take his revenge. It wasn't so much the language that he hated but the politics it represented.

'I know the accident killed your teacher, but what accident did you have?' Katya was looking down at his lifeless legs now.

'Nobody has ever asked me that question before'.

Finn wasn't being truthful. Perhaps, it was a question he had never answered before, not even to himself. A psychologist in the prison had visited Finn over a period of months. At the end of each session he had told Finn that there was no physical cause for his paralysis. The problem he had said lay elsewhere.

'I walked into prison a healthy man but the thought of the long prison sentence stretching ahead of me sent a message to my legs that they were not needed. As simple as that'.

He knew that his response to her question was glib and he also knew he didn't want to continue the conversation. A wound opened now that he thought had been lanced. He wanted to lift the atmosphere.

'Was there no help available to you in the prison, no physio? Nobody?'

'Enough now'.

She looked at him and he knew she wasn't prepared to leave the subject.

'What did you do all that time in prison?'

'I taught some fellow inmates how to read and write'.

Finn had assisted a literacy teacher in prison for the first year of his sentence while his appeal was being prepared. The lengthy process had been fruitless and the end result had left him in a state of lethargy.

'You must have been born to be a teacher, Finn. Did you teach them Irish?'

'No, they couldn't read or write in English. I'd been studying to be a teacher of English, not Irish. That's enough about me. You never mentioned your daughter before'.

'She's four and lives with my mother in Prague', Katya said, almost apologetically.

'Tell me more about her'.

'She loves mermaids. I told her on Skype yesterday that I saw a mermaid dancing in the sea outside the house where I'm living'.

Then Katya told Finn for the first time not only about her daughter but about the house she was staying in across the road, down a boreen leading to the Yellow Strand, and how she looked out to sea every night before going asleep.

'Please promise me one thing, Finn, that you will come with me to the Yellow Strand tomorrow'.

At the fall of night he went to bed with a fire in his blood. He tossed and turned and the image of the mermaid came to him, waltzing and twirling at the edge of the sea, inviting him to join her in the dance. He would drown in the water but if he could entice her to dry land he would help her find her legs. It would be painful for her, he knew that much. Making a gesture to invite her on land he held out his hand and moved his chair towards the waves and 'So help me God', he cried, feeling a current running through his awakening legs. The water sucked him down to her and his legs stretched out towards the illuminous creature. The tide pulled him around her and he was at last in tune with her rhythm. *Da, da, da, da, da, di, dum, di, dum ...*

The Gravel Road

It is early morning and a dog is barking in the distance; Georgina recalls hearing it at the same time yesterday. A knock on her hall door interrupts the sound. It is the first call on her front door since she moved into the house, three months earlier. Molly, her next door neighbour, always calls out to her over the back fence. Some people can be terribly informal.

The postman hands her two parcels, both addressed to:

Georgina Murray
The Innings
Mount Pleasant Avenue
Rathmines
Dublin 6.

A row of Argentinian stamps decorates the top of the bigger package. It is a shock to see her name written down; she has lived a life answering to two names and hasn't used this one for many years. The second parcel is the new millennium candle, sent to every household in the country.

She will open that one in a few months' time and light it to welcome in the New Year.

Georgina believes herself to be a woman not given to dreaming but, just this once, she allows herself a little pleasure. She places the bigger parcel on her breakfast table and tries to visualise the route of its journey. What countries has it travelled over? Would she ever see those places, now that she is in her fifties? Time, she has realised, is one luxury she doesn't possess, and she wants to spend it wisely. The parcel is now lying on her lap and she caresses it, wondering who might have sent it. She knows she is being foolish; it was she herself who ordered it from a website only two weeks before. She lets out a low chuckle – 'What sort of a woman are you?' – and opens the well-wrapped box. Red tango shoes are nestled inside bubblewrap.

She stretches out her slippered feet and walks to the hall mirror at the bottom of the stairs. Sitting down, she takes off her slippers and slides her feet into the red shoes. It takes her some time to gain her balance when she stands up. Studying her reflection, she notes that although the grey tracksuit bottoms do nothing for the elegance of the slender shoes, the high heels elevate her short stature. In the back of her mind she is already planning her new wardrobe, from the red shoes upwards to the crown of her grey hair.

The leaflet announcing the classes is waiting on the kitchen mantelpiece. It has been there for the past month – *tango classes for beginners.*

Tango wasn't part of the ballroom dances she had learned in that big room over the Stella Cinema. How long ago? She tries to push back the years. Lees of Rathmines was the big drapery shop across the road from the Stella – the Centra shop and Eddie Rockets diner are there now. Lees was where her mother took her to get her school uniform for Sandymount High School in the early sixties.

Navy-blue gymslip and primrose yellow blouse. Further down the road was the Monument Creamery where, as a young girl, she used to do errands for her grandmother when she visited with her father. Her grandmother's daughter, easy-going Margaret, was her favourite aunt. Margaret had worked in Rathmines Library and often, on her way home from Sandymount High School, Georgina would get off the number 18 bus and go to the library to see her aunt and do her homework.

Less than a year ago, a letter had arrived at her convent. 'Sr Gabriel, a letter for you'. It was always Sr Patrick, the oldest of the four remaining nuns, who distributed the post, and she had stood beside Sr Gabriel as she opened it. It was from a solicitor, a Mr Byrne, stating that Georgina was the sole inheritor of her aunt's estate, including the house at Mount Pleasant Avenue. There was a large sum of inheritance tax to be paid by the benefactor, but Margaret had left provisions for that in her various accounts, knowing that Sr Gabriel had no money, having taken a vow of poverty.

Her aunt's house had held many happy memories for Georgina. She remembered the long back garden, at the end of which was a small whitewashed wall overlooking a big cricket green. As a child, she'd loved visiting her grandmother and aunt Margaret there. After her grandmother's death, Margaret had stayed on. She had never married, but was happy with her life, content to spend her working days in the library. Margaret was an authority on children's literature, among other topics, and on many a visit, Georgina remembered her aunt not only reading stories to her, but also making up some of her own.

Georgina's father used to say, 'Fantasising again, sis, when will you ever join the real world?'

Margaret's reply was always the same: 'Whatever that is?'

The letter required Georgina to confirm her intentions in relation to the house. Did she want it to be sold and the proceeds to go to her account? There was no hesitation on the nun's part; her mind had been made up before the letter had even arrived.

It was a decision that had taken months of soul-searching. The order Sr Gabriel had entered all those years ago had had work for her, work which had involved the nurturing and education of children. But in the early eighties the convent building had been closed down by the Eastern Health Board and sold to a developer. The children had been fostered out to families and the nuns had moved residence, living in a group of small houses in the area. Sr Gabriel's reputation as a gifted teacher of special needs children had been well known in the community and the local school had offered her a teaching position. It was supposed to be a temporary role, but had lasted for nearly twenty years. When, in the late nineties, she'd finally been replaced by a young teacher, she had felt that it was time to review her life.

The timing had coincided with other changes. There had been no new vocations in the past twenty years and the convent community had now dwindled to four. The group of houses, now too large for the remaining nuns, were being sold to take advantage of rising house prices; the four nuns were being moved to a permanent home in Wicklow. But Georgina felt that she wasn't ready yet to be put out to graze. The century was coming to a close. If she moved to Wicklow, she knew it would mark the end for her; new beginnings were what she needed if she were to survive the coming years.

Her biggest regret would be parting with her friend, Sr Carmel. Over the past three decades, they had become inseparable, as much as the rules of the convent would allow. But Carmel, although only a few years older than Gabriel, was growing frail; unlike Gabriel, she welcomed the idea of the Wicklow convent as a resting place.

Months before receiving the solicitor's letter, Sr Gabriel had written to the Mother Provincial. She knew the words off by heart.

Dear Mother Provincial
It is with a heavy heart that I have decided not to renew my vows this year. I wish to live my remaining years outside the convent.
Yours faithfully,
Sr Gabriel, née Georgina Murray.

This letter had been lying unread in Sr Gabriel's drawer; she had known that her freedom from her vows would be immediate. Now was the time to send it.

It was a long time since she had been Georgina Murray – over thirty years. She would also write to the solicitor, and sign using that name.

Georgina places her red tango shoes in her bedroom, away from the prying eyes of her neighbour. Molly has developed the habit of calling to her over the garden fence most mornings since Georgina moved in. It's only been three months and the house is beginning to feel like her own, but she doesn't want to be spied on now that she is finally alone. Molly reminds her too much of the old days in the convent, the watchful eyes of the nuns.

Georgina walks into the living room cum kitchen, and surveys her favourite spot in the house.

'Oh, to have a little house to own, the hearth and stool and all'.

The words from a Padraic Colm poem, learned in her first year at Sandymount High School. Light floods the room. It is south-facing, with sliding glass doors opening onto the patio. Her aunt had been house-proud and kept up with the latest fashions of home improvements in the area. The beech wooden floor gleams like golden honey and Georgina shouts out loud with excitement: just the perfect surface to practise tango on. It's a good day to walk out.

Sliding open the door, she walks the length of the garden. 'This land is mine', she says to herself with every step, until she reaches the back wall which divides the garden from the cricket field beyond. Young boys are playing on the pitch. They ignore her. She sits for a while on the wall, watching them bat and bowl. The sound of the ball on wood is hypnotic. Children, they are a whole other world away. Or are they? She doesn't want to think about that. The morning sun is much warmer than she expected and she takes off her grey cardigan before making her way back to the house. The big blue hydrangea blooms near the sliding doors remind her of her childhood summers. They will have to stay where they are, she thinks.

'Hi Georgina, are you taking the air on this lovely morning? Would you like to come in for a cup of coffee?' Molly appears on the other side of the fence, interrupting Georgina's train of thought. But Georgina is not yet ready to be neighbourly. This is her space, hers alone, one where she doesn't have to account for her every waking hour.

'No, thanks, Molly. I've some business to attend to'.

Molly and her aunt Margaret were on friendly terms – according to Molly anyway – but people need to learn that Georgina is a different person entirely, not nearly as easy-going as her aunt. She notices Molly's eyes reflected in the glass as she slides the window shut. The thought strikes Georgina that she will have to work on a clearer code of behaviour with her next door neighbour.

Walking down Castlewood Avenue towards the closed Stella Cinema, Georgina turns right at the traffic lights. She heads down Rathmines Road, seeing as far as the Town

Hall clock on the right-hand side and, on the left, the library where Margaret used to work and the college beside it. It's a good feeling to know that some things remain the same. An optician's shop just before the library has taken the space of the Copenhagen Café, a place where Georgina had many a girly heart-to-heart chat with her school friends. They would sit over their coffees, dreaming about what they would be when they grew up, the juke box music playing in the background. When they had the money it was always Elvis: 'Blue Suede Shoes' or 'Love Me Tender'. But love wasn't something Georgina had thought much about in those days. The boys in her class were too childish for her. If she were to fall in love, she'd imagined, it would have to be with someone older, more mature.

The Red Shoes Café used to be tucked behind the Copenhagen; the luxury of having the choice of two coffee houses in Rathmines then was like being part of a Hollywood film set. The other well-known café was in town, The Amsterdam in Anne Street, and Georgina remembers being there only once, with her aunt.

The red shoes in her bedroom enter her mind again. She has to purchase something suitable for her first tango class tomorrow night. Oxfam is just ahead. Updating her wardrobe hasn't been an item on Georgina's agenda until now, but she knows she can't meet new people in a tracksuit. She needs to smarten up, to brighten up. Colour, she decides, is what is missing in her life.

Georgina Murray was eighteen years of age when she joined the convent. The choice was either a secretarial course or nursing after she had finished her Leaving Certificate. The film *The Nun's Story,* starring Audrey Hepburn and Peter Finch, was showing at the Metropole cinema in O'Connell St that summer and she became convinced that she had the 'call' to serve and save the world – perhaps in Africa or India. She had also thought that Peter Finch was the type of man she could admire.

There had been nothing to keep her at home. A few weeks after Georgina finished the Leaving Cert, her mother had had a heart attack. She'd collapsed in front of Georgina while they were cutting the grass. It all happened too quickly. Her mother had been taken to hospital in an ambulance and died within minutes of her arrival. Georgina had stayed by her side until her last breath.

'Be a good girl for your father'.

But seeing her mother die so suddenly had left a huge chasm. The house wasn't the same without her; there was nobody to talk to. Georgina's mother had always sat down at the table when her daughter came home and listened gently to the stories of Georgina's day. Now, though, her aunt Margaret was out of the country on a work exchange programme, while her father's personality soon became more distant. Weeks passed slowly as the summer progressed, and it seemed to Georgina like all her friends were starting to go out with their boyfriends. She felt that everyone she knew had abandoned her. The incident that brought things to a head was when Georgina saw her father in town with a young woman, much younger than her mother. She knew she couldn't stay in the same house. The pieces fell together: Peter Finch, *The Nun's Story* – the decision to join the convent was made.

Georgina entered the Sisters of Light. She understood that this order had several houses all over the world and she could see herself travelling across continents, learning new languages and living in a community with other sisters. An only child, she had always longed for sisters.

It is the day of the tango lesson, her first. The leaflet had stated: *Come early to register. Only 20 places available. Class: 8–9.30pm.* The Rathmines Town Hall clock chimes out four bells, but she has a lot to do. After her bath she blow-dries her short grey hair and notices the shine on the black strands on her fringe. She forces herself to look at her naked body, though she can't bear to linger over her protruding bits. The red trouser suit she had bought in Oxfam will conceal the lumps and bumps, and the white T-shirt underneath will, she hopes, create an air of casual dress. She decides to wear her flat black shoes and bring her red tango ones in a bag, just in case she doesn't get a place in the class. The dance studio is in Camden Street, only a short walk from her house.

On her way out the door, she bumps into Molly. 'All done up. I hope you're going somewhere nice? I believe they're starting bridge classes in the club tonight'.

Georgina looks at her watch. It's only seven o'clock; she is far too early. Perhaps she has time for a quick chat with Molly; it wouldn't do to be too unfriendly with her nearest neighbour.

'Good evening, Molly. Yes, I'm …'. Instinctively, she draws her bag closer to herself. There are some things she shouldn't have to reveal, not to a stranger. 'I'm going to meet a few friends'.

'You must come in for lunch one of these days. We've hardly had a decent chat since …'

Molly stops herself, but Georgina knows exactly what she means: since the convent.

She looks away. Her glance alights on the blue lobelia plants in Molloy's front garden. Her eyes feast on the colour; she had never realised it was so vibrant. 'I love that colour, Molly. How would you describe it?'

Molly looks for a moment at Georgina, as if she doesn't know what way to take the question. 'Cobalt blue'.

Georgina quickly says her goodbyes and walks down the road, over Portobello Bridge, towards Camden Street. She feels like she is walking towards a wonderland that might transport her to new heights. Stop dreaming, girl, what are you like? Both these thoughts are pulling against each other in her head as she approaches the door of the dance studio. She puts her hand to her forehead to straighten her fringe and feels the little beads of perspiration. The stairs up to the first floor are dark and steep. At the top, a dark-skinned man is sitting behind a table.

'Good evening, you are the first?'

His voice is deep. She has never seen a man like this at such close quarters. He is dressed in a tight-fitting sleeveless top and she can see his well-defined biceps as he stretches his arms wide in a greeting motion. Maybe she's made a mistake in coming here. Should she pretend she has the wrong address? But before she has time to speak, a young man wearing glasses arrives up the stairs behind her.

'I hope you're here to join the class. It's my first time too'. He holds out his hand. 'My name's Tony'.

Tony, she guesses, is in his thirties. He's only here as a means of keeping fit, he tells her; he's tired of gyms.

'Me too', she says. She is pleased to discover an excuse for being there. Soon others arrive in dribs and drabs and by eight o'clock the studio is full.

The dark-skinned man is called Sydney and he turns out to be the teacher. He tells the class that he is from Argentina but has travelled all around Europe. Ireland is now his home. He seems to be happy, now that he has his full quota of twenty students, all paid up and registered. Georgina looks around the group and decides that she is not the oldest; she is relieved to see the age gap isn't too dramatic. Men and women in their forties, fifties and maybe even sixties; it's so hard for her to tell exactly. There are also some very young people, perhaps in their twenties.

'I'll start gently tonight. First we'll do warm-up exercises. Then I will play the music and we will take our partner and embrace the first steps into the tango'.

Sydney looks at Georgina and she feels her face burning. They walk around the room in a circle and listen to the music. She finds it difficult to do the warm-up exercises as her trousers are too tight. Next week she will make sure to wear something loose, something she can stretch in.

Georgina walks home with a much lighter step. After making herself a cup of tea, she goes upstairs and prepares for bed. Earlier in the day she had cleared a shelf in her wardrobe for her red shoes. Before she draws her curtains, she looks across the cricket green and beyond to the two red and white twinkling Poolbeg towers. The lights are still on in the clubhouse. One of these days she will investigate what goes on there. Didn't Molly say something about bridge? But right now the tango music is echoing in her head and her body feels like it has learnt new moves. She recalls one of the warm-up exercises from the class; sweeping the right leg back as far as possible. The trouser suit had restricted her earlier. Now, though, she puts her heart into the movement. Trouser suit or not, she would not have allowed herself to move like that in the class.

She stretches out in bed. The tiredness in her body is a source of pleasure to her. Sydney, the teacher, comes into her mind.

'Listen to the beat of the music. Feel it'.

She dreams she is dancing close to Sydney; she is listening to his melodious voice, his face is close to hers and she feels the heat of his chest. He is pulling her closer and closer, and what is more, she is enjoying the sensation and is wanting more. He is saying: Let the man lead, follow my movements. She feels herself getting carried away as he places his face close to hers, his chest against hers, and then she hears the voice of Mother Evangelist shouting at her:

'You are making an unholy disgrace of yourself, Sr Gabriel! You're as bad as the young girls here that have given in to sins of the flesh. Do you not realise you are a daughter of Christ and that you have taken a vow of chastity?'

Georgina wakes. It takes her some time to realise it was a dream.

Mother Evangelist wasn't a dream, however, and neither were the young girls who were housed in the convent where Georgina would spend all of her youth and most of her maturity. Georgina never travelled to Africa or India; in fact, she never travelled outside of Ireland. The convent was known as the Mother and Baby Home in Dublin; Georgina used to think it was like a baby farm. The day she had first arrived at the big hall door would seem like a fairytale to her older self. She would find it impossible to recognise the part of herself who had been that girl. Her father had driven her and she had taken all her possessions from the house she was reared in; she no longer thought of it as home. A new life had been ahead of her.

The driveway in was long and twisted and the screech of the car wheels on the gravel marked the moment of her entry. She wondered, briefly, if she was making a huge mistake. The big red-bricked house was concealed by large trees and hidden away from the outside world. It was new territory to Georgina, although it was only a mile from the city centre. The northside was a foreign country to people from the southside.

She stopped her father knocking on the door. 'It's best if we say our goodbyes here'.

He said he was sorry for the way things had turned out and that if she ever wanted to change her mind, her room would always be there for her. But one thing Georgina was sure of, and that was that she would never return to that house again. They shook hands and Georgina saw that her father was crying. He handed her a wallet of money.

'This is for you and not the nuns'.

She looked after him until the back of his car was out of sight and then she knocked on the big hall door.

A young nun answered. She had an open, smiling face. That was Georgina's first impression of the convent, mixed in with the smell of frying rashers and lavender polish that had hit her when the door opened. The young nun introduced herself.

'Sr Carmel'.

She was a little older than Georgina.

'Mother Provincial is having breakfast with Fr McCarthy and she'll meet you in the parlour shortly'.

Carmel guided Georgina into the front parlour, where a highly-polished table stretched the length of the room. Over the high marble fireplace was a portrait of a saintly man with a strange hat on him. She thought of her father going back to his new life, his new woman who was soon to become his wife, and wondered what her mother would have made of this sudden turn of events.

Voices in the hall were getting louder.

'We do our best, Fr. See you again tomorrow, please God'.

A small nun entered the parlour. She seemed around the same age as Georgina's mother, but her brown eyes frightened Georgina; they were cold, like searchlights looking for its prey.

'So you're about to become our new postulant'.

Her tone was very different to the one she had used with the priest.

'I'm Mother Evangelist, your Mother Provincial. You are very welcome to St Philomena's'.

After writing down a few details in a big ledger, the small nun picked up a bell and shook it. Sr Carmel appeared.

'Will you show our new girl to her room and introduce her to her new surroundings'.

Mother Evangelist looked at Georgina and a glimmer of a smile appeared in her eyes.

'You're so young. We will see you later at Vespers and, in a day or two, we'll introduce you to your first programme of spiritual studies, along with the other new postulants'.

Sr Carmel carried her suitcase for her. They walked to the back of the main house and up two flights of stairs that led to a long corridor, off which lay the small bedrooms where the nuns would sleep. They passed several small wooden doors on the left; the walls on the right were covered with pictures of saints. They came to the last door.

'This is your room'.

Sr Carmel opened the wardrobe. Inside were hanging two navy-blue dresses, only a little different to the gymslip of Georgina's school uniform.

'Your aunt posted them to the convent, along with other items, so they'd be here to welcome you on your arrival'.

Georgina remembered Margaret's last letter, sent to her father's house just before she had left for the convent.

'You won't be needing your civvy clothes in here, so I'll put them away for you'.

Georgina handed over everything to Sr Carmel, including the wallet of money her father had given her.

'Very good, Georgina. You'll be taking the vow of poverty, so there'll be no need for money here. I'll give everything to Mother Evangelist'.

Later that evening, after Georgina had changed into the navy-blue dress, Sr Carmel knocked on her door.

'I'll bring you to the church and you can join the congregation at Vespers'.

They walked across the garden to the church on the other side of the quadrangle. Georgina was surprised to see a nun with a white veil standing outside the door, holding a broken vase in her hand.

'She's been proclaimed against at Chapters and this is her penance', whispered Sr Carmel.

The church was full. Georgina followed Carmel to the front, passing pews filled with nuns in black and white head-dress. The white-veiled novices were in the middle section and the postulants filled the front rows, their heads covered with black lace mantillas. The sound of the organ echoed through the church. After singing a hymn that Georgina didn't know, some nuns led the prayers.

A professed nun with a dark veil stood up and in a loud voice sang out.

'I proclaim on Sr Monica. She was singing on the altar this morning during her task of cleaning and broke one of the holy vessels through her negligence'.

The unfortunate Sr Monica, the nun Georgina had seen with the broken vase outside the church, walked up and stood in front of the congregation. 'I accuse myself of breaking silence in the house of God'.

Georgina was shocked; this humiliation was like a child being sent to Dunce's Corner.

After Vespers, Sr Carmel walked Georgina back to her room.

'There will be Profound Silence from now until dawn. It'll be broken at five o'clock by the bell for Matins, followed by mass at seven. Sleep well, Georgina'.

The next day, Carmel took Georgina on a tour of the grounds. Outside the main house were other buildings. One was a hospital wing where the girls had their babies. Beside that were the girls' living quarters, the nursery, where Sr Carmel worked, and the adjoining changing rooms to cater for the babies' needs. The sleeping area for the girls, little cubicles very close to each other, lay right beside the nursery. On the other side of the girls' quarters lay the orphanage.

The orphanage would be Georgina's first workplace in her early weeks of entry to St Philomena's; it was here she would first meet Ruth. Both girls had arrived at the convent on the same day, both eighteen years old. Ruth was eight months pregnant and was hiding in St Philomena's until the birth and adoption of her baby. Her pregnancy had been the result of an affair with a married man. Although Georgina was not yet ready to admit, the reason she was there was also because of a married man: her father.

Georgina wakes up hungry the following morning; must be the extra energy she'd used the previous night during her tango lesson. Porridge is her usual dish in the morning, but today she decides that she'll change her routine – perhaps toast and a boiled egg instead. The freedom of choice is beginning to excite her; it is giving her new energy. In the convent she had to eat whatever was presented to her on the table. As well as her food, her daily routine had also been programmed. Most days it was silent prayers at five o'clock, followed by mass. Breakfast at eight, laundry duties, then teaching in the orphanage.

She sets the table and places one of the blue hydrangea blooms from her garden in a small vase. Out in the garden, she notices a magpie scratching away in one of the geranium flower pots.

One for sorrow.

She wasn't ever superstitious. Wherever there's one bird, another is bound to be nearby, just around the corner. A pity, she muses, it isn't the same for us humans. What can be around the corner for her, at her age? At least she has her health; she is lucky to be alive, and fit. She intends to get even fitter, fitter for the next tango session.

The next class is a few days away and she knows that she can't wear the same constricting clothes. The vibrant cobalt of Molly's lobelias and the muted azure hues of her aunt's hydrangeas waft together and she feels her spirit rise. Black and white was all she had been accustomed to during those years in the convent. Now it's time to get an injection of colour back into her bloodstream.

Nothing too expensive, though. Money is scarce with her. After she was professed as a nun, she had to make a will, signing all her earnings over to the order. The wallet her father had given her when she'd entered St Philomena's had never been mentioned after that first day. The convent had taken it from her, along with all the clothes and possessions she'd brought with her. Like all the other nuns, Sr Gabriel had received no pay for the work she did in The Gravel Road. Later, during the years when she taught in the local school, her salary was paid directly to the convent and she was given only a small weekly allowance.

Now a weekly stipend from her aunt's inheritance just about puts food on the table. It will be another fourteen years before she is eligible for the state non-contributory pension. Will she have to consider the question of work? There are plenty of schools in the area and she has ample teaching experience. This new boom has been good for jobs.

She will think about those matters later. For now, another shopping trip is due. Going back to Oxfam in Rathmines is not an option she wants to pursue, so she sets off to walk towards town. Walking, she decides, will help keep her fit.

Molly is sweeping her front path as Georgina leaves her house. 'Off again?'

Georgina feels a flush of irritation. This is nearly as bad as the convent, having to account for every movement. In fact, it's worse; in recent years, the few remaining nuns of what had once been The Gravel Road had shown no interest at all in the outside world. Not even Carmel, God bless her. But Molly is becoming an annoyance; she is beginning to upset Georgina with her constant questions.

'I've business to attend to, Molly. It's of an urgent nature'.

It's not good to let people like that get into your head.

'In that case I'll leave you to it, Georgina'.

Now Molly doesn't sound quite so friendly. Perhaps Georgina has gone too far. Was she rude? She forces herself to smile at her neighbour before walking on down the path.

She'll invite Molly to her house in a day or two, she decides, try to undo her harsh words.

In the convent, friendships among nuns hadn't been encouraged; in fact, they had been strenuously discouraged. Older nuns spied on younger nuns and kept records of their daily activities. Carmel and Georgina were often accused of 'breaking silence' during their work period and were proclaimed against at Chapters. Proclaiming had taken place in a small room in the convent. Once a week, nuns openly confessed their sins to the congregation; any person who failed to confess was later proclaimed against by a professed nun. There was always a penance, which involved standing outside the church at Vespers. On many an occasion as young nuns, both Gabriel and Carmel had to stand in front of the congregation and speak out.

'I accuse myself of breaking silence'.

Mother Evangelist had many spies.

Pulling her bag over her shoulder so that her arms are free to swing by her side, Georgina sets off towards town. She recalls all the points of her first lesson. Press into the balls of the feet. Sydney had said that good footwork depended on strong ground contact through the balls of the feet.

'They are the fulcrum point, the fixed point of balance'.

An image of his strong thighs comes into her head and she walks even faster, not taking much notice of where she is going. The way to town is easy for her. These streets are her territory – though she can count on one hand all the times she had been allowed out into the city during her years in the convent. There was a course she'd attended after being professed, in St Patrick's Teacher Training College. She would get the bus there and back. And every summer she would travel by train to Kerry for two weeks, to St Philomena's summer house. Carmel and herself would swim every day and walk to the local village.

'Shoulders down'. Her shoulders are stiff, tense. 'Chin forward, leaning towards chest, and mouth relaxed, forehead relaxed'.

Sydney's voice, deep and caressing. A tingle of excitement stirs somewhere in her body, but she is not sure where. There is work to do physically. Relaxing isn't easy for her; she knows she has to learn to let go.

Grafton Street is round the corner, all changed since she was a girl; pedestrianised, British chain stores. Thank God Trinity College looks the same.

The biggest surprise is when she comes into Abbey Street. While it's good to see that Wynne's Hotel hasn't changed at all, it's a shock to see the lovely China Showrooms replaced by a tatty euro shop and a Centra supermarket, and the banks which have been turned into public houses offend her. Boom-time Dublin is not a pretty sight. She can't remember the last time she was in this part of the city. Even the Abbey Theatre looks different. She loses count of the number of people who ask her for 'change'.

Oxfam in Talbot Street is empty when she arrives. She takes her time searching the rails, looking for something that will take her fancy. A new colour is what she wants; blue, it has to be blue. A dress or a skirt would fit the bill. Her legs are slim, the slimmest part of her. She sees a blue skirt on a figure in the window, the same cobalt as Molly's lobelias. It reminds her of her favourite skirt as a girl. It had been a blue taffeta flowing garment that ballooned out like an opened umbrella when she twirled. She had worn it to a few tennis hops in Leinster Cricket Club when she was still a schoolgirl. She now has a hunger for that very colour; she has to have it.

'Seek and you shall find'.

She needs something loose, leggings or a light garment that won't interfere with her movements. She can't see herself in leggings, but perhaps a loose pair of blue cotton trousers would be the next best thing. She finds a pair of blue trousers that fit and is pleased by her reflection.

A letter is waiting for her in the hall when she opens the front door. The writing is familiar. It's from Sr Patrick, one of the three remaining nuns from the Wicklow house, the convent's final residence after The Gravel Road. Sr Carmel has died.

'The house is like a mausoleum for dying nuns now', writes Sr Patrick. There is only herself and Mother Evangelist left, and Mother Evangelist is as difficult as ever, worse now that she's slipped into senile dementia.

Carmel had been Georgina's friend; the one person who had helped her during her Noviate years and all the years that followed, those long years when they had worked like slaves from early morning till late into the night for absolutely no money. On the day of Georgina's Noviate ceremony, it was Carmel who had cut her hair and helped her to put on the white veil. That was the day she became Sr Gabriel, her new name chosen for her by Mother Evangelist. By chance, it was that same day that her father married his new wife. The invitation to the wedding had arrived weeks before Georgina's ceremony and had been opened by Mother Evangelist. Nothing got past her eyes, not even the reply that Georgina sent to her father, saying she could never see him again.

It had been Sr Carmel who had helped her cope with that grief, the loss of both her parents. The sense of emptiness on the day of her ceremony wasn't about her long ponytail collapsing to the floor, but something much deeper; her sense of a profoundly confused identity.

Carmel was only a little over fifty, not much older than herself. Life is short, thinks Georgina and there is so little of it left.

The funeral takes place two days later in Wicklow. A handful of people sit in the small convent church. The only people Georgina recognises are the two elderly nuns, Patrick and Evangelist. The priest officiating speaks about Sr Carmel.

'She was an angel on this earth and her place in heaven is waiting for her'.

Georgina finds herself crying. This young priest was a far cry from Fr McCarthy, who used to say mass in The Gravel Road and was wined and dined in the warmth of the main house each morning. During Georgina's first weeks in the convent she had been assigned to help the cook and they would set the silver tray for his breakfast and listen to the chat between the priest and Mother Evangelist, his account of his intimate conversations with the pregnant girls. She wondered if he knew how often the girls complained about him to Carmel.

Georgina walks over to the two old nuns and holds their hands. They smile at her and, for a moment, she wonders if they recognise her.

'You managed to get away'.

It is a long time before Sr Patrick lets go of her hand. Yes, she thinks to herself, but I should have left much sooner, twenty years sooner. Why did I leave it so long to come out? Silly question. She knows the answer. Weeks turned into months, months into years, time flowed by like the river outside the convent on The Gravel Road. There was so much to learn during those days. The children needed her. Her spiritual path was a long journey and she had always believed that God had chosen her for that road. Both she and Carmel had been convinced that their purpose in life was to save and protect children in their care.

Then that day, out of the blue, she didn't see it coming, the Health Board closed down the orphanage and placed all the children into foster homes. Gabriel was suddenly redundant. So too was Sr Carmel. The Mother and Baby Home had ceased to be. Was this when her vocation had begun to erode? But that was eighteen years ago. Why had it taken her so long to leave?

On the bus home, Georgina can't get the funeral out of her head. 'Going Home' had been the last hymn to be sung. But what do nuns know about home? 'Community' was always the term used to describe a family of nuns; a congregation contained under the same roof, abiding by the same set of rules, governed by a Mother Provincial, who in turn was governed by the Archbishop of the Dioceses, who in turn was answerable to the Pope.

Poor Carmel had stayed until the end, the final end. Yet she had seen lots of beginnings, more beginnings than any mother in Ireland. She had been the nun in charge of the nursery; that room as big as an acre, full of new babies, fresh flesh waiting to be planted in new families, new homes. Gabriel's place of duty had been the orphanage; children awaiting adoption who had been turned down because of imperfections, deemed less than ideal for the family market. The first time Georgina visited the nursery, she'd found it a huge contrast to the bedlam of the orphanage. It had reminded her of a big field of freshly fallen snow; white cots lined up in perfect straight lines, row after row of freshly-ploughed land waiting to be sown. Each cot identified with the name, date of birth, and weight of baby as they entered this world; labelled and marked.

Ruth, the pregnant girl who had arrived the same day as Georgina, had had her baby in the nursery. Georgina had been forbidden to have anything to do with those girls.

'You're becoming far too familiar, Sr Gabriel. Remember, you are a daughter of Christ and these girls have fallen from grace, they have sinned'.

The biggest and only sin in Ireland at the time had been sex. Ruth had stayed with her baby girl for six weeks. After the birth, she had been given tablets to dry up the milk in her breasts and her baby had been taken to the nursery to join the queue of other infants.

Twice a day, the young mothers had been allowed to come to the nursery, pick up their babies and take them to the feeding and changing room. After changing their babies, the girls would sit in a circle, bottle-feeding and cooing at them as if they were dolls. Sr Carmel and Sr Gabriel used to watch this ritual without a word. They had known that if they'd spoken to the girls, they would be proclaimed by the Mistress of Novices at Chapters.

Yet it was impossible to always keep their distance. The father of Ruth's child had come to visit once; Ruth had wanted him to see the baby.

'*His* baby', she had cried out to Gabriel. 'He didn't even ask to see her'.

Visitors weren't allowed in the nursery, but Gabriel asked Carmel to turn a blind eye to his visit. Carmel had pretended not to see, but later she told Gabriel that he had lifted the baby out of the cot and kissed her. Then he had gone home to his wife.

Soon after that, a family had come to take Ruth's baby away. They drove up the long gravel driveway and left the convent shortly afterwards with the infant in their arms. Ruth and her friends had looked on from the balcony as the car drove away, to a destination that Ruth would never know. Back then, it was an occasion of joy when a girl's baby was placed; it meant that the orphanage was not going to be the final home for the child.

Ruth had been free to go after that. She had returned home to her parents, with some cock-and-bull story of travels abroad. Weeks after her departure from St Philomena's, Gabriel overheard a phone conversation in Mother Evangelist's office.

'If you don't stop whinging, Ruth, I'll have the baby sent to your parents' doorstep'.

Evangelist had slammed down the phone.

'That'll give that young girl something to think about'.

Gabriel had been stuck to the spot in the doorway of the office, unable to move one way or the other.

It transpired that the baby had been adopted by a relative of Mother Evangelist, but the legal documentation had yet to be signed by Ruth. It was a dilemma for the convent. Mother Evangelist was a wise woman in such matters. She had her relative send a photograph of the happy baby; this in turn was sent to Ruth, with a request that she attend the solicitor's office and sign away her right to her birth baby.

Those girls had thought they were free, but it was only in years to come that they would realise this experience would plague them for the rest of their lives. Gabriel was to have many a visit from girls, not just Ruth, seeking to have their babies back.

It is the day of the second tango class and Georgina has butterflies in her stomach. The blue trousers are laid out on her bed and a navy-blue short-sleeved top will create a slimming effect. Georgina is considerably happier with her appearance than she'd been a week earlier.

A dog barking somewhere outside the house takes her attention. It is very nearby. She looks out her bedroom window; the dog is in her garden, a small Jack Russell, running around in circles. She goes downstairs and out into the kitchen and the dog continues to bark, his head looking in her direction. He seems to be talking to her from the other side of the window. She freezes. She has had no experience of dogs in her life before; not at her parents' home, nor in the convent. She plucks up her courage and tells herself not to be such a coward and, after a few seconds, slides the door open.

'I'm terribly sorry'.

A man is on the other side of the back wall that borders the cricket green. He looks to be in his late fifties.

'I don't know how the little rascal got over your wall. We used to visit the previous owner during the summer. It's force of habit, I think'.

'My aunt Margaret?'

'Yes, that's right. I'm Bernard O'Brien, here to watch the cricket. May I climb over and get JR?'

He jumps into her garden.

He tells Georgina that he lives on the other side of the green. Each year he takes two weeks' holidays to coincide with the cricket matches; aunt Margaret used to mind his dog while Bernard sat on the bench, on the other side of the wall.

'Forgive me for disturbing your peace. I'll take this little fellow out of your way'.

Just as he's about to climb back over with his dog under his arm, he stops.

'Do you ever visit the clubhouse? You're almost on its doorstep'.

Georgina is surprised by his direct question but finds herself looking him straight in the eye.

'Perhaps I will, one of these days'.

'You'll be more than welcome. It's a very friendly place'.

She remembers Molly saying that they play bridge there. Perhaps bridge might be her next project. One thing at a time. It's a pity, she thinks, they don't give dancing lessons there.

The music is playing as she climbs the stairs. A few people are sitting on the long bench at the side of the room. Georgina sits down and says hello. Sydney comes over as she is changing into her red shoes.

'Have you done much dancing before?'

The other people stop what they are doing and wait for her response.

'Well … yes and no'.

Sydney looks at her.

'I did some ballroom lessons when I was a young girl. Of course, that was a very long time ago, but nothing since'.

One of the young girls beside her looks over.

'Oh, why? That's a shame that you gave up so young. You've great rhythm'.

Georgina can't make out if the girl is sincere or if she's making fun of her. Whatever the case, she doesn't want to go into her life story with this stranger.

'I was away for many years and it wasn't possible'.

Sydney smiles at her.

'Well, let's make up for lost time. Here, in this room, we can take flight in any direction'.

He holds his hand out to Georgina.

'Come with me, I want to demonstrate a classic posture, with this classy lady who knows the rudiments of old-fashioned dancing'.

He sweeps her up and down the studio room, and calls out to the class.

'Head up, shoulders down and own your own space. Stop, start and change direction. Hold yourself upright'.

Tony arrives a few minutes late and Sydney gently guides Georgina towards him.

'Your partner for the rest of this dance'.

At the end of the class Tony waits for her to change into her walking shoes.

'I'm going your way – that is, if you're not doing something else'.

'Oh no, I'm nearly ready now'.

She feels like the best girl in the class.

'You know, at the end of this course, we're invited to do a Milonga in the Tapas Bar across the road'.

'What's that?'

'It's dancing the tango around the tables as part of the diners' entertainment'.

'I don't think I'm ready for that yet'.

Georgina smiles at Tony. She feels like she is young again; not quite a girl, but light of heart.

When Georgina arrives at her house, she discovers that her key isn't in its usual place, in her purse. She'd changed her purse before leaving so it would match her new outfit; she must have forgotten the key. This is her worst nightmare. Now she'll have to knock on Molly's door.

'Thank God you're in, Molly', she hears herself saying. She sounds almost hysterical. 'I've lost my key'.

'Oh, let me see. Yes, I've Margaret's spare here'.

Molly holds out the key. Then her stiff expression softens.

'Why don't you come in, Georgina? The *Late Late* is on'.

'I really wouldn't like to disturb your programme, Molly'.

Georgina is embarrassed at the memory of their previous conversation, how rude she was.

'Nonsense, Georgina. I'm delighted to see you. Come in, please'.

Making an effort, Georgina steps over the threshold and into her neighbour's house. It's the first time she has been there.

'Please, sit down'.

The two women sit in silence for a while, not paying much attention to the chatter of the television. Georgina can't help but notice the photographs on the mantelpiece.

'You have a big family, Molly?'

'Six grandchildren now. But unfortunately none of them live in Dublin. They'll be visiting here in a few weeks and I can't wait to see them. You'll have to meet them'.

As Georgina gets up to take a closer look at the grandchildren, her bag falls to the floor. Molly picks it up.

'My dancing shoes, Molly'.

The words are out of her mouth before she can stop herself. She stares at the floor. She can sense the critical eyes of Molly burn into her. It feels like being proclaimed all over again. But then she looks up and sees the expression on Molly's face.

'I'm happy for you, Georgina'.

Molly's eyes are full of sympathy. 'You've missed out on so much in your life. It'll be a race now to catch up'.

Georgina is furious with the uninvited flush to her cheeks.

Georgina can't sleep. Her secret is out. She wonders what she should accuse herself of now, like she and Carmel used to do in The Gravel Road. Is it a sin to want to enjoy a little dancing in life? She is only fifty-two and feels that she is still in her prime. But the years in the convent had been fuelled by guilt; it will take her some time to rid herself of that dark mantle. Before settling into a disturbed sleep, she thinks of Molly. Will it be possible to see her with friendlier eyes? She promises to make amends to her neighbour.

Then she remembers Bernard. It's always a person's tone of voice, a person's body language, that she notices, not so much their apparel. He had a nice voice; rich, resonant.

The following morning, her kitchen is filled with light, so much so that she thinks she has left a switch on all night. It is one of the things she loves about this house.

She is about to make coffee when a knock on the front door disturbs her. Checking herself in the mirror, she runs her fingers through her short hair. She wishes she could smooth out the wrinkles under her eyes, push back the clock a few years.

There is no dog this time. Instead, his arms are cradling a stack of books.

'Just want to return these to their rightful place'.

'Bernard. Please come in'.

She makes them both coffee and they sit in the kitchen, watching the men in white warming up before the match.

'A great day for cricket', is all she can think of saying.

'Yes', he says. 'Myself and your aunt used to have long discussions over these books. Margaret was a mine of information on the Second World War. She spoke a lot about you too'.

Is this his way of saying that he is familiar with her background, that he knows she used to be a nun?

Georgina is a little lost for words. 'Where's your dog today?'

'JR? My next door neighbour's looking after him. But he's going away for a few weeks tomorrow'.

Georgina sees herself, walking out with a dog; it could be another useful way to keep fit.

'Bring him over tomorrow. I can do with the exercise'.

Bernard walks out to the garden shed.

'You don't mind if I open this door?'

'Please do. I haven't got around to it yet'.

There is a big dog's dish on the top shelf, alongside tins of dog food. He takes the tins off the shelf to examine them.

'Still in date'.

They say their goodbyes. He walks down the garden and leaps over her back wall, into the cricket field. He turns and waves.

'See you tomorrow, Georgina'.

She looks at him go. Then she dances back into her home; into her favourite room, filled with light. Her feet tango: three steps forward and three steps back. She has the hang of it now. Swivelling her head to repeat the steps, she could swear she sees a reflection of a ponytail brushing across her shoulders. Time past and time present, she thinks; and she holds the image together.

ACKNOWLEDGEMENTS

My sincere gratitude is due to the many people in my life who walked the road with me during the making of these stories. The idea of writing this collection came about as a result of the M.Phil in Creative Writing in Trinity College, Dublin during the years 2007 and 2008. Susan Knight's classes in 'The Short Story and Beyond' in UCD in 2005 got me started. Celia de Fréine, life-long friend; her work ethic and friendship has inspired me to continue. The people who read first drafts and inspired some of these stories: Sile Agnew, Colette McAndrew, Rupert Jenkins, Ann Murphy, Ruth Webster, Betty Thompson, Bernadette Sproule, Monique Walsh, Fíona Bushe, Paddy Bushe, Irene Brady, Katherine Graham, Carmel Lynch and Sibylle McGovern. My sister Eileen Graham for her cover art and her insightful reading of final drafts. My brother Eamonn Herbert for his good-humoured support and belief in me. To Mia Gallagher for her astute editing. To Adrian Kenny and Jack Harte for their endorsements. Finally my thanks to Alan Hayes of Arlen House for taking a chance in publishing my first collection of stories.

About the Author

Phyl Herbert was born in Dublin and has worked as an English and Drama teacher in the Prison Schools and in Liberties College, Dublin. During those years her creative interests in education were mainly in the use of drama in the curriculum. Concurrent with those teaching years, Phyl trained as an actor and director with The Focus Theatre, Dublin, under the late Deirdre O'Connell.

In 1988 the Curriculum Development Unit at Trinity College published her first book, *Role Play and Language Development* with illustrations by Martin Fahy. Her second book – a collection of plays written with Celia de Fréine – *Literacy, Language, Role-Play* (Sarsfield Press, 1990) was published in response to International Literacy Year and was grant aided by CDETB. Mid-way through her teaching career she did a Masters in Drama in Education in 1982 with Dorothy Heathcote at Newcastle-Upon-Tyne University.

Emerging writers are not always young in years. After her teaching career her interest in creative writing grew. Susan Knight's class at UCD introduced Phyl to the art of writing. In 2008 she completed an M.Phil in Creative Writing in Trinity College. Her work is published in the anthology *Sixteen After Ten*. Phyl has broadcast essays on radio over the years and her stories have been shortlisted in literary competitions. This, her first collection of short stories, was longlisted for the Kate O'Brien Award and the Edge Hill Short Story Prize in 2016.